JOE HALDEMAN

MORE WILDSIDE CLASSICS

JOE HALDEMAN

by

JOAN GORDON

WILDSIDE PRESS

For my father,
Mordecai H. Gordon

JOE HALDEMAN

This edition published in 2006 by Wildside Press, LLC.
www.wildsidepress.com

CONTENTS

CITATIONS AND ABBREVIATIONS

Because science fiction tends to go in and out of print frequently, I cite chapters rather than page numbers. These citations will occur parenthetically in the text and will use the following abbreviations.

AMSR   *All My Sins Remembered*
FW   *The Forever War*
ID   *Infinite Dreams*
MB   *Mindbridge*
WY   *War Year*

Most of my research into Joe Haldeman's ideas about his writing come from the most logical source, namely the author himself, through correspondence and taped interviews he and I conducted. Quotations from these sources are indicated parenthetically in the text by (interview, date) or (letter, date).

I.

CHRONOLOGY OF LIFE AND WORKS

Joe Haldeman is in the midst of a very successful career in science fiction. He is best known for his first science-fiction novel, *The Forever War*, which was critically and financially successful and paved the way for further successes, including his finest novel to date, *Mindbridge*, and his financial, if not artistic, success, *All My Sins Remembered*.

1943   Born in Oklahoma City, Oklahoma, on June 9.

1949   Moved to Anchorage, Alaska.

1951   Started reading science fiction in the third grade.

1952   Moved to Bethesda, Maryland. Had a poem published in the *Washington Post*.

1961   Began college at University of Oklahoma.

1963   Transferred to University of Maryland, majoring in physics and astronomy.

1965   Married Mary Gay Potter, August 21.

1967   Graduated from University of Maryland with B.S. in physics and astronomy. Wrote "Out of Phase" and "I of Newton" during his last semester for a creative writing class. In September, he was drafted.

1968   On February 28, sent to Vietnam. While there he wrote a column, "Notes From the Jolly Green Jungle," for fanzine, *ODD*. On September 14, severely wounded in the Central Highlands. Hospitalized until February 1969.

1969   Honorably discharged from the army. Spent the summer in Mexico. First story, "Out of Phase," published in September issue of *Galaxy*. Also in September began graduate work in computer sciences at University of Maryland.

1970   Attended Milford Conference in June, dropped out of University to write full-time. *War Year* accepted and short stories selling regularly.

1970-1972 Treasurer, Science Fiction Writers of America (SFWA).

1971   Moved to Florida where wife Gay taught high school to support his writing. Began *The Forever War* in the spring. Published "To Fit the Crime," first novella of *All My Sins Remembered*.

1971-1972 Taught short story writing for Hernando County Adult Education. Wrote Attar adventure novels.

1972   Wrote "Fantasy for Six Electrodes and One Adrenalin Drip," the script for a "feelie," to be published in Harlan Ellison's *Last Dangerous Visions*. "Hero," the first part of *The Forever War*, published in June *Analog*, received Hugo nomination. *War Year* published in September.

1973   *Study War No More* submitted in January (accepted July, 1976). Also in January, "Time Piece" published in French in *Galaxie*. *In a Vision Once I Saw* submitted in March (accepted in different form as *Infinite Dreams* in November, 1977). In July moved to Iowa City, Iowa, and joined the University of Iowa writer's workshop. "We Are Very Happy Here," also part of *The Forever War*, published in November *Analog*. *The Forever War* accepted.

1974   *Cosmic Laughter* published. "The Only War We've Got," second part of *All My Sins Remembered*, appeared in January *Galaxy*. *The Forever War* finished in May. In summer, toured Europe. Began *Peacemaker* (which became *Mindbridge*) in September.

1975   *The Forever War* published in January, with "End Game," part of the novel, appearing in January *Analog*. Taught "The Science Fiction Novel" at University of Iowa during spring. Received M.F.A. in English from University of Iowa in May. Finished *Mindbridge* in November. Attar books published under pseudonym Robert Graham. Senior editor, *Astronomy* magazine, during December.

1976   Wrote "Tricentennial" in February, published it in July *Analog*. In March, guest of honor at Marcon, his first GoH of many. In April, *The Forever War* won Nebula. *Mindbridge* was published and *All My Sins Remembered* was accepted for publication. In June, Avon bid $100,000 for paperback rights to *Mindbridge*, the highest paid so far for science fiction work. In September, *The Forever War* won Hugo and Ditmar awards. *The Forever War* published in French edition. *Planet of Judgment* published.

1977   Moved to Ormond Beach, Florida, during the summer. "Tricentennial" won Hugo in September. Paperback of *War Year* with original ending restored published. *All My Sins Remembered* and *Study War No More* also published.

1978   Last Star Trek novel (*World Without End*) finished in May. Went to

World SF Meeting in Dublin. Began *Worlds* in August. Worked on non-fiction work, *The Endless Horizon. Infinite Dreams* and *World Without End* published.

1979   During May went to Los Angeles, California, to write script for Space Pavillion at Disney World in Orlando, Florida. During August and September, attended World Science Fiction Convention at Brighton, England, and toured England and France. In fall, finished *Worlds* and installed computerized text-editing equipment in home.

II

INTRODUCTION

The Beginning

"Tonight we're going to show you eight silent ways to kill a man." This sentence introduces the protagonist of *The Forever War* to a harsh new world. Joe Haldeman had first heard this sentence in basic training, and for him, it marked a disturbing and destructive confrontation with war and the relent-lessness of government. For Haldeman, this confrontation was the catalyst for some of his best writing.

Haldeman's childhood was stimulating and varied, and it provided en-couragement, if not subject matter, for his science fiction. Haldeman, whose father was in the Public Health Service, was born in Oklahoma and lived as a child in Puerto Rico, New Orleans, Alaska, and, less exotically and for longer, in Bethesda, Maryland.

His most vivid childhood memories seem to be of Alaska. Many of these memories are of horrors: the pet bear that clawed his mother and later ended up on an autopsy table, a woman who threatened his father with a knife in the family living room, men with .22's hunting feral dogs in downtown Anchorage. More numerous, though, are memories that show an intelligent child in a stimulating environment: Joe watching his parents developing photographs, his mother reading aloud to him and his older brother Jack, his father making up stories about Muffindragons, his own voracious appetite for reading, his writing of stories and one-page cartoons, and a burgeoning interest in astronomy.

In Bethesda, which was then slower and more rural than the cement-en-crusted and automobile-infested suburb it is today, Joe gave lectures in science and philosophy "to the local kids for a dime apiece (Koolaid supplied free)" (letter, November 14, 1978).

"Around about eleven or twelve I got fascinated with chemistry and had a laboratory in my bedroom until I was 18, and left for college. My parents were amazingly patient with the explosions and fires. About the same age I went into amateur astronomy with a real passion, saving up enough to buy an eight-inch reflector, which I observed with almost every night.

"And I was writing. For some reason plain fiction didn't appeal to me. I wrote several books of poetry, most of it lyric poetry in standard forms. I also wrote novels (" ") [Haldeman's odd punctuation stresses the unusual nature of his cartoon strips] in the form of cartoon strips forty or fifty pages long. I drew a lot and painted" (same letter as above).

From these childhood memories, Haldeman reveals how science and writing had always occupied him, partly because of the encouragement of his parents, partly because of his own intelligence and character. But there were a number of directions his life might have taken, given these factors. He might have become a poet, a cartoonist, or an artist. His college degrees were in physics and astronomy: a career might have offered itself in one or both of these areas. Instead he combined science and art with his fondness for science fiction and his desire to entertain and make a mark. He began to write science fiction.

That fondness for science fiction began in the third grade with *Rocket Jockey* by Lester del Rey and *Rocket Ship Galileo* by Robert Heinlein. "And my doom was sealed. I read nothing but science fiction and science until puberty struck . . . . Science fiction was my main diet up through the first couple years of college" (letter, February 6, 1979). It is not uncommon for science fiction to visit one as a driving obsession and it so visited Haldeman. Before he had ever written a science-fiction story, he had done a great deal of unprogrammed research in the field. Though not, perhaps, on a conscious level, he sensed what had been done, how, and by whom.

While at college, Haldeman changed from a solitary reader to a part of the social group of science-fiction fans.

"My first brush with fandom was the 1963 Worldcon in Washington, but both Gay [his wife] and I managed to wander through the long weekend, thoroughly enjoying ourselves, without getting a clear idea of what fandom was, and without realizing there was a large SF club in Washington, sponsoring the show. A year or two later we did make connections with WSFA (Washington Science Fiction Association), through the girl who later married my brother (I met her at a govt [sic] and politics class; she saw my copy of *Analog* and struck up a conversation to avoid a guy who was bothering her; as sweet a piece of cosmic whimsy as can be). By the time we graduated (and I was drafted) in 1967, fandom made up the bulk of our social life— It still does" (same letter as above).

Fandom swept him up as science fiction itself had. Here were people who shared his reading obsession and who shared other interests as well. Joe plays guitar and sings; fandom enjoys "'filksinging," folk singing with science fictional or fannish lyrics. Both Haldeman and his wife are shy people who blossom in a warm atmosphere; fandom asks only shared interests to provide a welcome. And when Haldeman began to publish science fiction in 1969, fandom was full of friends who were also experienced and interested readers of science fiction.

The Lessons of War

By the spring of 1967, during his last semester of college at the University of Maryland, Haldeman had written two science-fiction stories—"Out of Phase" and "I of Newton"—but they weren't published until two years later. His writing career was interrupted by the Vietnam War. In September of 1967 he was drafted, five months later sent to Vietnam, and on September 14, 1968, severely wounded.

"I was never sympathetic with the army. They wouldn't let me be a conscientious objector because the conceit that I was morally opposed to killing people meant nothing if I was an atheist . . . . Went to war and went to the army anyhow. Tried to make the best of bad lot. By that time I was pretty well convinced that I would at least be a part-time fiction writer and I thought this would be a good experience" (interview, June 6, 1978). If "good" meant that his time in the army would trigger much of his finest writing, then Vietnam was excellent experience. That he would pay so dearly for his material was not something he had planned. Haldeman's own description of his most dramatic Vietnam experience reveals how shattering it was.

"We were doing a fairly routine job, my outfit. We had overrun a North Vietnamese encampment and chased them all away. There were very few casualties . . . . There had been some fighting and we were with two companies, about 250 guys, and they were tired. We had been moving and we found this thing . . . a conical pile of high explosives in the middle of everything. It's called the DX pile. Any time some explosive seems untrustworthy, wet or something like that, we give it to the engineers and they make a pile and when you leave the outfit you just blow it up where it is.

"They hadn't blown this up and an obvious ploy is to booby trap it. We told the infantry that we thought the thing was booby trapped and they should all move out and let us blow it up. They said no; these boys are tired; they've been fighting and walking for a long way. Let them stop and rest for awhile first. Seemed reasonable.

"We stood guard around it and to this day I'm not really sure what happened. But trying to reconstruct it, it seems to me that one of the guys picked up a piece that looked like a rifle grenade but it was really bamboo with wire wrapped around it and it had Chinese characters on it which made it a real collector's item. We were passing that around and I gave it to a guy named Farmer. Then the artillery cook, who was about ten meters away, who knew us all, said, 'Hey, don't give that to that turkey, he'll drop it and blow us all away.'

"And my back was turned, but what soon happened was that Farmer threw it away. And it went off. Just to get the guy's goat.

"Anyway, about half of this booby trap went off. Well, it involved about a ton of high explosives. It was enough to blow a whole company away. And it killed everybody else. But me. And it hurt me pretty badly. I had over 200 wounds.

"But I don't know. If I had—I put myself in the position of the enemy. They had an hour or two hiding. I would have made what they call a command detonator and waited until there were a maximum number of people around it and set it off.

"And that may be what happened. I don't know. When the thing blew off, it knocked me over and everybody started shooting. Nobody knew what had happened. Thought we were getting mortar rounds, artillery rounds, into the camp. Everybody flopped down and started shooting. And I was trying to get a medic and my medic was virtually dead. Had both his legs blown off—in the blast. And the artillery medic came over and he saw that I was more or less intact and he went over to the other guys. It was a pretty significant thing to happen" (same interview as above).

It was a significant thing to the man and to the writer. Explosions, shooting, violence, maiming: those will appear in *War Year, The Forever War, All My Sins Remembered,* and all the war-related short stories. Even now, Haldeman is planning at least one more novel on the theme, a mainstream novel with the working title *1968,* told from the shattered viewpoint of a schizophrenic Vietnam war veteran. Yet the violence and personal destruction are only a part of it. "The actual experience of the army was more important to my work than the experience of war" (same interview). Haldeman learned much from that explosion: the suddenness and unexpectedness of fate, the dislocation which imminent and ubiquitous death must cause, the power of a single image or sequence of images, and his own fragility and mortality. Yet he could say that the everyday realities of army life taught him more. He learned that:

(1) Life is episodic and without patterns for an individual to rely upon;

(2) An individual is in the snare of an organization characterized by the motto SNAFU;

(3) An individual is a pawn in the government's game and his fate is out of his own control;

(4) Soldiers are considered by the government to be not people but counters—a dead soldier takes only one counter off the board but a wounded one takes two;

(5) To the government, and eventually, to the individual, a person *is* his profession, no more;

(6) An individual is expected to fight to save a culture which has changed and forgotten him while he was absent from it;

(7) An evil individual can win, at least temporarily, within the amoral and amorphous government . . . morality guarantees nothing;

(8) An individual will find himself repeatedly, yet willingly, taking orders from people who are his inferiors;

(9) He will take orders, whether they are right or not, because survival depends upon acting as a group;

(10) Sent to war by a government, an individual fights not for politics but to save his own life and the lives of his buddies; and

(11) An individual lives only to get through a few months or a few days; goals become smaller and nearer in threatening times.

As the government seeks to make an individual less a human and more a mechanical tool, an individual learns to see himself and his narrow group of buddies as very human and very important. Some of Haldeman's lessons—living for short-term goals, recognizing a chaotic world—are the same ones the existentialists postulate. Others, such as the willingness to obey incompetents and to work in a group and the recognition of inherent evil in certain people and actions, are something else again. Whatever the philosophy these lessons reflect, they show a grim tangle of a world, a world that becomes the locale of Haldeman's frequently autobiographical fiction.

On the other hand, the situation of imminent death can encourage a sense of perspective and need not stifle a sense of humor. Joe Haldeman managed to survive the war with all his senses intact, and the same man who anthologized alternatives (not necessarily improvements) to war in *Study War No More* also anthologized humorous science fiction in *Cosmic Laughter*. Though many of his stories are of the inward and outward maimings by war and government, Haldeman sees other worlds besides the world of military combat. He also writes of knowledge and exploration and craftsmanship and morality in any endeavor, and he recognizes that any career may be as soul-sucking as the army.

Milford and Beyond

The Milford Conference was an annual occasion, meeting at Damon Knight and Kate Wilhelm's home in Milford, Pennsylvania. A congregation of published writers, famous or not, spent an intensive week together, reading and criticizing one another's stories. Haldeman attended in May, 1970.

"Present at the conference: Bova, Dickson, Ellison, Laumer, Knight, Wilhelm, Wolfe, Budrys, Spinrad, Russ, [Carol] Emshwiller, plus about a dozen of us non-famous.

"These were the rules: a schedule was posted; everyone to read each day's stories well ahead of time. In the morning and afternoon there would be round table discussions; starting on the author's left, each person would discuss the story without interruption for ideally, less than ten minutes. After the story had passed around, the author was allowed time for a finite rebuttal. Everybody [would] show up promptly at 10:00; break for cold-cuts around noon . . ., try to finish before dark. No friends or spouses allowed in the meeting room. Every rule save the last one was more-or-less broken . . . .

"It's no exaggeration to say that the 1970 Milford totally changed my life. Mostly the people. The final effect was that I left with a sneaking suspicion that I could write science fiction for a living" (letter, February 21, 1979).

"Mostly the people." This is what had drawn Haldeman and his wife to fandom, too. In neither case does the strength lie so much in contacts (though they are made) or in particular advice or responses from readers: writers are too independent. The strength lies in warmth, support, a feeling of community, commitment, and possibility. Today Haldeman is what he had a sneaking suspicion of becoming: a professional writer. He and his wife have a home base in Ormond Beach, Florida. Joe writes, Gay handles the business, and their many friends in science fiction come to visit.

In Florida, Haldeman has a rather Spartan work schedule. The particulars are subject to change without notice, of course, but at the moment they are something like this: he gets up at three or four in the morning, runs or bicycles, gulps down lots of coffee and then sits down to the typewriter for six or seven hours. There he thinks through each sentence slowly and carefully, editing it in his memory, and then types it, seldom doing many drafts because the editing in his head is so thorough. By lunchtime his writing day is over, and he can spend the rest of the day at leisure. Leisure includes handling personal and organizational correspondence. He deliberately breaks this schedule for about three months of the year, simply to keep his sanity. The discipline seems to work. Haldeman writes and publishes steadily, has many future writing projects planned, and has not yet let his vision of disorder and violence lead him to a writing block.

He has come a long way since Milford, from a beginner learning the trade to a new professional in science fiction. His science-fiction novels are always reviewed, and usually favorably, in the science-fiction magazines; wherever they appear, his short stories and novellas draw many readers; he is guest of honor at many science-fiction conventions, and he has received two Hugo awards and one Nebula award. He is well known and well respected. The list of his accomplishments is quite impressive for an author yet to reach his creative stride.

III

WAR YEAR

Though Joe Haldeman had already published six science-fiction short stories and novellas, his first published novel, *War Years*, belongs to the mainstream. It is a first-person narrative of a young man's initiation into war, career, and life. The book is largely autobiographical in its sources and contains much that would become characteristic of Haldeman's science fiction in content, style, and theme. Haldeman directly confronts his experiences in Vietnam, experiences which affected so much of his later work.

Its Making and Publishing

While Haldeman was at Milford, he told Ben Bova, a science-fiction writer and editor, that he wanted to write a novel about Vietnam. Bova suggested Haldeman make it a "young adult" novel and offered to help get it published. After Milford, Haldeman sent Bova the first two chapters of *War Year* and an outline of the rest of the novel, and Bova wrote to his editor at Holt, Rinehart and Winston, recommending the book for their Pacesetter series.

"This series was a selection of novels on adult themes written in simple English, mainly for adult education reading classes .... They were also marketed to libraries as young adult category fiction. Holt accepted *War Year*, but not as a Pacesetter. They attempted to market it both as a regular novel and as a Young Adult" (letter, February 1, 1979).

Because Haldeman had to shape his novel to a specific program and audience, he didn't have an entirely free rein on the shape it would take. He had to limit vocabulary and keep sentence structure simple, while keeping the action on the upswing and the philosophy to the minimum. All these would make the novel accessible to "young adults" and to adults with poor reading skills. He chose a narrator that his readers could readily identify with without feeling threatened: John Farmer, an antiheroic, uneducated greenhorn. Readers sensitive to their own shortcomings would be much more receptive to a character like themselves than they would be to an intelligent, well-read college graduate like "the Professor," who is Haldeman's autobiographical character. The rites of initiation and passage, in this case into war, are successful themes for initiates, the young or poorly educated readers of *War Year*. These restrictions were very appropriate to Haldeman's intent to generate a curt, hard, and realistic look at the Vietnam war. Using spare language and an ordinary protagonist, he could do so.

One other restriction did not suit Haldeman so well. When he submitted the original manuscript, it ended with the narrator's death by a grenade in Chapter Thirteen and a last chapter (fourteen) of less than a page, told in the third person, limited to the viewpoint of an army captain who is about to notify Farmer's mother of her son's death eight hours earlier. The editors objected to this unorthodox killing of the viewpoint character and, perhaps, to the downbeat ending, so Haldeman changed it. The Holt, Rinehart and Winston edition contains the revised ending in which Farmer is injured in Chapter Twelve, and is back home again, cynical and directionless, in Chapter Thirteen, the last chapter.

Whether or not the editors wanted the ending to be more cheerful, Haldeman didn't really comply. Farmer does not make a hero's return by a long shot. However, keeping Farmer alive to tell his tale avoids the illogicality of a story told by a dead man. In January of 1978, after Haldeman had made a name for himself, Pocket Books published a paperback edition of *War Year* with Haldeman's original and preferred ending. There was one other request for plot adjustment with which Haldeman complied—the request to kill off "the Professor." Haldeman found it an odd sensation, killing himself off halfway through the novel, but he did and that change stuck in both editions.

Some confusion was caused by marketing *War Year* as both a young adult novel and as a regular novel. Haldeman uses much of the strong language and violence that he encountered in Vietnam. They were part of his attempt at an accurate view of the way things were. But library journals that received review editions labeled "young adult" were upset by the obscenity and violence. They thought it inappropriate for the tender young reader. *Library Journal* (15 September 1972, p. 2960) found the gore and profanity gratuitous and objected as well to what it believed to be poor characterization. *Booklist* (15 September 1972, p. 86) and *Best Sellers* (15 June 1972, p. 15) also objected to "a profusion of barracks language" or "repetitious verbal vulgarity," but they found the characterization and the view of army life convincing and were able to give the book a strong recommendation. George Davis, in *The New York Times Book Review* (21 May 1972, p. 8) gave *War Year* a review that was, on the whole, quite favorable, although Davis was puzzled by the publisher's decision to market *War Year* for young adults. Nevertheless, *The New York Times* selected *War Year* as one of the outstanding children's books of 1972 (15 October 1972, Part II of the review, p. 26).

In spite of a rather misleading cover illustration and blurb on the paperback edition, which imply that the novel is about a future war, *War Year* is indubitably a mainstream novel, dealing with the recent historical past as we know it. The time is 1968, the place is Vietnam, the situation is war. Haldeman expends his descriptive energy in the reproduction of the real and present world rather than on the invention of a new one. The creation of a strange environment had been done for him by the army. His characters are fictional adaptations of himself and the people around him. Because Haldeman wanted to write directly about what Vietnam had taught him, both to clarify the experience for himself and to teach others vicariously, the logical medium was an autobiographical mainstream novel. Because the experience itself needed examination and exorcism, Haldeman couldn't translate it to another time and place. Once he had taken these steps, translation would follow and add new insights. But not this early in his career.

Partly Truth, Partly Fiction

Part of the effectiveness of *War Year*, as both didactic writing and entertainment, is due to its being based on real, observed events.

"*War Year* isn't really autobiographical although the minor character Professor is loosely modeled after me. I suppose it's technically a realistic, or naturalistic, novel informed by autobiography. Every major incident except for the final scene [Farmer's death] in the paperback edition happened during my year in combat, either to me or to someone I'd talked to.

"The main character Farmer bears a physical resemblance to a real person named Farmer, but the resemblance stops there . . . .

"My idea for the novel was to make Farmer an "everyman" draftee— anything that could happen to an unwilling soldier happens to him, including sudden death. My initial plan was to follow an *In Cold Blood* pattern and structure the novel directly after what had happened to my unit during the year I was in Vietnam, using my diary as the main source (I wrote Gay every day, and she kept the letters in order for that eventual purpose). It was obvious, though, that I'd have to switch the chronology around to make a novel of it. It's still historically accurate in detail and setting, though the order of settings doesn't follow the actual movements of the 4th division in 1968" (letter, Feburary 21, 1979).

Farmer does have two autobiographical links with Haldeman, though a lanky, naive, and poorly read innocent like Farmer is more striking for his departure from the original. Haldeman, like Farmer, was designated a demolitions expert though he had been on "KP" when it was taught during basic training (interview, June 6, 1978). This example of SNAFU at work suggests the second similarity: Haldeman gives his narrator his own view of a military too unwieldy, impersonal, and single-minded to cultivate personal integrity.

Appraisal

War Year is an apprentice novel, and a novel written partly to accommodate an editor's set of rules: in these facts lie its strength and its weakness. Haldeman turned his restrictions and simple language, combined with compelling action and a narrator who is accessible to slow adult readers, into the appropriate tools for the story he wished to tell. There is no room for misunderstanding the harsh presentation of reality as it is set before John Farmer. He could not miss it and neither can the reader. The starkness of the novel's language reflects the barren ground of war and the impoverished individuality of the soldier. Farmer's own experience and education reflect what Vietnam and army life did to the individual and exemplify the typical victim.

Emphasis on action rather than thought makes the novel accessible to poor readers. It does other things as well. It illustrates how army life (indeed the lives of most career-oriented people) consists predominantly of actions, leaving little time or energy for the examined life. And it encourages an episodic structure that strings many actions together without imprinting an order on them. This is the way Haldeman sees reality, as a string of events lacking the orderliness of traditional plot structures. Even John Farmer's death (in the original manuscript and paperback edition) is less a climax than just the end of his rope. And it is of no greater order of significance than an unpleasant and awkward detail in the life of the officer who must announce the news of his death to the boy's mother. Instead of finding them a burden,

Haldeman has recognized and used the restrictions of a "Pacesetter" novel to strengthen and confirm his direct description of the way things are.

The novel does have gaps of credibility—and because credibility is so important to the effect, *is* the effect—the gaps cause a troublesome injury to the book. What is the book's intended audience? The tone is that of a letter home (not surprisingly; that was the form of Haldeman's diaries), yet Farmer is an inarticulate young man accustomed to written words no more dense than the balloons in his comic books. He wouldn't write his story; he would tell it. This would work since there is much speech in the novel's style, except that there is no one for him to talk to. Most of the time we are caught up enough in the story to accept the fact that we are his audience and that there is no fictional one, or that we hear Farmer's subvocalized monologs on events as he experiences them; once in a while, though, the language may stutter a bit: a phrase awkwardly repeated, an inconsistency in the grammar, a description of gore which almost lapses into inappropriate humor. We become aware of the difficulty and realize that this in some ways still the work of a journeyman who is not yet master of his craft.

Some examples will substantiate the stuttering. In Chapter Two, two paragraphs begin "It was" and the repetition seems careless. Later, in Chapter Six, the narrator speaks of "chunks of bodies we had to gather up onto a poncho and dump them into a hole." This isn't his characteristic use of grammar, and it causes the reader to become aware of a certain lack of control. The sentence fragment which follows is in powerful contrast: "Man-shaped charcoal lumps, feather-light, burned crisp by napalm." There is no lack of control in that painfully precise line. In Chapter Thirteen of the paperback, the gore briefly lapses into jarring humor: "I squashed an eyeball with my elbow."

War Year as a Barometer

War Year is atypical of Haldeman's work in that it is not science fiction, but it still contains much that is representative of Haldeman's style, content, and themes. He writes the novel in a style that has much of the oral story-teller, albeit a very careful and precise one. He uses a document (the list of army issue equipment in Chapter Four) to lend authenticity, as he does even more frequently in later work. The influences of Hemingway and Crane are quite strong. Like Crane in *The Red Badge of Courage*, Haldeman looks directly at the horror of war and its terrible beauty through the eyes of an initiate. Also, like Crane, there is a real sense of the malicious playfulness of Fate. Haldeman's emphasis on action over abstraction, his use of stark language and the sequence of motion and fact, and his tracing of a young man's attempt at grace under pressure show Hemingway's influence. As Haldeman more solidly develops his own style and views, the direct influence will diminish, and Crane and Hemingway will become precursors rather than influences.

Though *War Year* is not science fiction, it employs techniques which Haldeman later applied to the genre. He is able to insert naturally into the story the necessary explanations for alien concepts and objects. He revels in accuracy of technology as he does in his hard science fiction and uses scientific method and careful observation in *War Year* just as he does in *The Forever War*.

IV

THE FOREVER WAR

It is the year 2007 and a brilliant young man is drafted into an elite army to fight a war against bug-eyed monsters from a distant planet. Space ships, monsters, strange weapons, and heroic soldiery are the all-too-common framework of space operas, those horse operas of the sky, but Joe Haldeman uses this seemingly uninspired framework to build a sound and aesthetically satisfying edifice, *The Forever War.*

The content of *The Forever War* has two main sources, one used consciously, the other not. Haldeman made a conscious application of his experience in Vietnam to this future war. Unconsciously, he found inspiration by reacting to Heinlein's initiatory future war story, *Starship Troopers.*

The Forever War, which successfully combines adventure, social comment, speculation, and a convincing love story, turned Joe Haldeman into a famous man in science-fiction circles. Before the publication of *The Forever War* in January, 1975, he was publishing science fiction steadily and successfully. He had a personal bibliography of thirteen short stories, seven novellas and novelettes, a novel, an anthology, and a play. He had received a Hugo nomination for "Hero" and had had three of his short works translated into French for *Galaxie.* But the critical and financial sucess of *The Forever War* made him a major name in the science-fiction market. The novel won the Hugo, Nebula, and Ditmar awards; sold very well; and made it economically possible for Haldeman to retire from his assistantship at the University of Iowa and from "one excruciating month" as senior editor of *Astronomy Magazine* (letter, September 15, 1978). Since January of 1976, he has made his living entirely by his writing.

Its Anthologizing and Publishing

Haldeman began writing *The Forever War* in the spring of 1971. He had discovered a character in his story "Time Piece" who was too appealing to be dropped and who grew to be William Mandella in the novella "Hero." Twenty pages into the writing of "Hero," Haldeman found that Mandella and his world would soon grow beyond the novella into a full-fledged novel.

With the structure of the novel in his mind (though the original outline apparently has little resemblance to the final novel), he completed "Hero" and sold it as a novella to *Analog*, where it was published in a much edited form in the June, 1972, issue. Later, in November, 1973, came "We are Very Happy Here" that would become "Sergeant Mandella" in *The Forever War*, in November 1974; "This Best of All Possible Worlds" that would become "Lieutenant Mandella," and in January, 1975, "End Game" that would become the last part of "Major Mandella" in the novel. Haldeman did not write these three novellas and then turn them into a novel, but rather he created an episodic novel that lent itself to serial publication. This practice—publishing a novel first in serial form in one of the science-fiction magazines—is not uncommon in the field and the reasons for it are quite practical; the author is paid twice for essentially the same work: first for each novella and then for the novel, and the potential audience for the novel is increased by serial exposure.

The practice has its disadvantages in the power exercised by the magazine editor and in the critical accusation that often follows: that the novel is just a bunch of stories stapled together. Joe Haldeman worked under at least one of these disadvantages. Though he and *Analog's* editor, Ben Bova, got along quite well, were great friends in fact, and respected each other as professionals, Bova's tinkering with Haldeman's book, done to suit *Analog's* projected readers, was not entirely to Haldeman's taste and often seems to me ill-advised. In "Hero" (later "Private Mandella" in the novel), the tinkering consists primarily of cleaning up barracks-room language (something the library journals had longed to do for *War Year*), making the narration a bit less colloquial than Haldeman had written it, and changing the paragraphing. These changes neither improve nor greatly alter the work.

"We Are Very Happy Here" (later "Sergeant Mandella" in the novel), in addition to the sorts of changes mentioned above, contains a more serious alteration. In the section where Marygay is seriously injured by her pressure suit, perhaps the most powerfully written passage of the novel, Bova has done a good deal of altering for *Analog*. The fragmented sentences reflecting Mandella's state of mind were eliminated and flat narrative was substituted, and the empathetic care that Estelle Harmony, one of Mandella's former lovers, takes with Marygay, his present and deeper one, was replaced by the regulation procedures of an army doctor. These substitutions significantly injure the power of the writing.

Thirty-eight pages of "Major Mandella do not appear. The result is that much of the personal, romantic, and sexual life of Mandella is missing from the magazine. There is, however, an interesting addition to the *Analog* version. Our cloned descendants want to replicate Mandella for his barbaric killer instincts. He declines: his war lust has been knocked out of him. Perhaps this scene made his anti-war stance too obvious for Haldeman's liking—it isn't necessary to an understanding—but it is an effective coda to Mandella's military career and seems worth keeping for that reason. The additions, subtractions, and alterations that Bova made collectively downplay Haldeman's harsh frontal look at the horrors and depersonalization of war and tend to skirt the intimate side of Mandella's character. They are not fatal to the book, but they often damage it.

While his themes and style were sometimes too extreme for a basically conservative magazine such as *Analog*, Haldeman's episodic structure lends itself to adaptation as a series of novellas. Haldeman chose episodic structures for at least three of his novels because he believes such a structure reflects exterior reality: "certainly life is episodic. In terms of drama, life is nothing but episodic . . . . There are no patterns you can rely on. And sometimes literature imposes patterns that are esthetically pleasing but it doesn't have to" (interview, June 6, 1978).

The Forever War, when it was published as a novel in 1974, earned praise from most of its reviewers, with the *Booklist* reviewer predicting correctly that *The Forever War* would receive the major science-fiction awards. Consistently cited were the book's realism and "gritty" view of army life (shades of *War Year*). Also praised were the clarity of the science and Haldeman's new stance on what are viewed as traditional science-fiction assumptions about the glory of war and the subjugation of women. Actually, there was only one negative review, in *Publisher's Weekly* (28 October 1974, p. 43), which dismissed *The Forever War* as "murky reading."

Objective Realism and Scientific Method
in *The Forever War*

Although science fiction deals with worlds created in the author's imagination and intellect, it must not project a baseless hallucination but should generate careful observation of objective reality. The narrator of *The Forever War*, William Mandella, is an intelligent and clear-sighted participant and observer: although he has a very personal stake, his own life, and a definite bias in his disapproval of much that makes up army life and the social situations in which he finds himself, he is a reliable witness. We see all events through his eyes, filtered through his emotions, but there is no doubt that events took place as he describes them or that his emotional responses are appropriate. The world he lives in may be an extrapolated creation of the author's imagination, but it is not a figment of Mandella's. The rat in the psychology experiment does not know the maze is artificial. Further, though Haldeman has made up this world and is not attempting the predictions of futurology, he is describing possible futures in as realistic a way as he can. In this way, their reflections upon contemporary life, whether as parallel or as warning distortion, are sharp and clear.

Mandella has a personal life, with individual problems, but this individuality is less important than what he represents. Mandella the individual loves Marygay Potter the individual, likes chess, comes to like at least one cat though he is not a cat person, dislikes leadership, and distrusts homosexuality. But his representative life is stronger. He is a man torn from every emotional attachment he makes by the relentless machinery of government, he is a victim of and a participant in pointless warfare, he is an alienated observer of a world much changed in his absence, he is a heterosexual in a homosexual world, and a man born of woman in a world of clones. Finally, he is a weary and retired warrior, able at last to settle down to a life that moves only at the normal pace. Thus he represents man uprooted from his individuality and his emotional life by societal pressures, man at war, man caught in future shock, man unable to conform to societal expectations (the heterosexual of the future might then represent the homosexual of today), and ultimately, man at peace.

Haldeman uses concrete, contemporary colloquial English free from metaphysical (as opposed to illustrative) metaphors and ambiguity of expression. He presents a series of specific images, events, and episodes that draw us to inevitable conclusions about the way the world works. Our lessons are of two sorts: we actually learn science when the narrator explains about collapsar jumps or the physics of acceleration, and we learn vicariously many

27

of the lessons Haldeman learned about war, as we follow Mandella's future history.

Haldeman uses computations, scientific terminology, and plausibly precise descriptions of his science. While a professional physicist would find Haldeman's science superseded or unspectacular, he would not find it careless. "I do make a lot of calculations but most of them are 1960's physics, and they're consistent within what I know to be true" (interview, November 1, 1977). Haldeman's careful science, as well as his scientific language, convinces the reader of the objective reality of the world he describes. At the same time, it teaches some of his readers a bit more about science. Haldeman says that his main aim in the careful hard science he employs is not to inform the reader but that "it's an exercise in convincing myself that what I'm writing about is possible" (same interview as above). He attempts to create, for the duration of each novel, an objective reality that is a logical extension of our present reality.

To teach and convince us of his world, Haldeman sometimes explains his science using the casual language of his protagonist:

> Just fling an object at a collapsar with sufficient speed, and out it pops in some other part of the galaxy. It didn't take long to figure out the formula that predicted where it would come out: it travels along the same "line" (actually an Einsteinian geodesic) it would have followed if the collapsar hadn't been in the way: until it reappears, repelled with the same speed at which it approached the original collapsar (Section 2, "Private Mandella," *FW*).

Such casual language, alien to textbook science writing, but consistent with the character speaking in the novel, distracts us somewhat from the fact that what Mandella says here is, nevertheless, a large gobbet of educational, not plot-forwarding, information, what Samuel R. Delany calls the "expository lump." The casual language also serves to make the explanation more easily understood and, hence, more entertaining. Even if we are aware of the expository lump here, we don't mind.

And we may become aware that the plot has halted to expose us to a necessary, albeit entertaining, lesson in science. Haldeman has other techniques, without this flaw, for teaching science. Sometimes he shows Mandella thinking through a scientific problem to solve it. At one point, Marygay is injured, and Mandella must think of ways to allow her to withstand the pressures of acceleration in her injured state (section 5, "Sergeant Mandella," *FW*). Mandella's thinking advances the plot; he is puzzling over a way to save his lover, and it teaches us about acceleration by leading us through Mandella's problem solving. This is a smoother way over the expository lump than the unemotional presentation of possibilities.

Haldeman is less interested in teaching us science than he is in teaching us about our society. The science makes us (writer and reader) believe the world: then we will believe the validity of the social situations we see enacted there. Here is where he most frequently applies the scientific method. Each episode of the novel works as a run of the experiment. Take the characters through this set of circumstances: what does it show about life? Now take them through another set: does it show the same thing, or a corrolary of it? Each episode acts as a successful replication of the experiment, showing the validity of its hypotheses and conclusions. There is even a control—one man, William Mandella, run through the variables: the year 2007, the year 2024, the year 2389, the year 2458, the year 3143. And we, experiencing and reacting to the forever war, replicate the experiment once more as we read.

Haldeman's use of the sequence of motion and fact is a kind of scientific method. He presents us with a series of images or events, and these specific steps lead us to a conclusion. "Elementary, my dear Watson," as that famous practitioner of inductive reasoning would have said. After a few vivid examples of pointless injury (Marygay's caused by a poorly fitting suit), death (those of soldiers who refuse to obey Mandella's orders), and anguish (Marygay and William forced to serve in separate campaigns for no reason beyond rigidity), we are led to certain conclusions about army life.

Haldeman had, in *War Year*, presented one document to substantiate his objective world. In *The Forever War*, he makes more extensive use of documents for this purpose, as well as for didactic purposes, showing us how the bureaucracy is organized, how it makes its decisions, and how tiny the place of the individual is within the vast organization. *The Forever War* contains five documents: two tables of organization, an order, a probability chart, and a news report. These documents, like illustrations, complement without interrupting the flow of the fiction and add solidity to the world the fiction presents.

In the novel's battle scenes, Haldeman simply shows technology at work. We learn how and why the weapons function through demonstration, and the demonstration furthers the action. In the same way, we learn how the concept of time dilation works by watching its demonstration on William Mandella. What could have been a dry exposition of the conditions of Mandella's own world is made vivid and convincing because it affects characters with whom the reader is emotionally engaged.

Subjective Realism

To say that we are convinced of the objective reality of *The Forever War* is not to say that the inner life is nowhere to be found. We are seeing the world through the eyes of William Mandella, and while he is a reliable observer, he reacts to what he sees. Sometimes his language reflects his state of mind. When he describes violence that he, unconditioned, abhors, his language may become hard-boiled and methodical as he relives the experience while trying to control the emotional upheaval it caused. Or he may lapse into a lyrical sequence which is a written equivalent to film director Sam Peckinpah's slow motion scenes of violence, forcing us to see with disturbing clarity the horror Mandella has experienced. When Mandella describes Marygay's injury, he cannot cut off his emotions nor can be look squarely into the horror: his sentences fragment and snatches of conversation interrupt descriptions.

And Mandella dreams. Early in the book, if you want consistency, I should have put (Section 10, "Private Mandella"), he dreams that he is a machine, "Mimicking the functions of life, creaking and clanking my clumsy

29

way through the world." Much later, after he has survived (barely) a particularly bloody battle, he describes the scene in the ship's infirmary, where he has just awakened from the anesthesia:

We were being ignored by the ship's two doctors, who stood in bright light at operating tables, absorbed in blood rituals. I watched them for a long time. Squinting into the bright light, the blood on their green tunics could have been grease, the swathed bodies, odd soft machines that they were fixing ("Lieutenant Mandella," *FW*).

In both these passages, we enter into Mandella's inner life but in these, as in other instances, the exterior world elicits the responses.

And Mandella thinks. He and Haldeman offer us a view of objective reality, but they both know enough about Einstein and the toll of army life to understand that our hold on objective reality is a tenuous one.

The collapsar Stargate was a perfect sphere about three kilometers in radius. It was suspended forever in a state of gravitational collapse that should have meant its surface was dropping toward its center at nearly the speed of light. Relativity propped it up, at least gave it the illusion of being there . . . the way all reality becomes illusory and observer-oriented when you study general relativity. Or Buddhism. Or get drafted (Section 10, "Private Mandella," *FW*).

Initiation

The Forever War, like *War Year*, is an initiation story, although the initiation of *The Forever War* is more complex. In *The Forever War*, a young man is initiated into the army, an adult into a brave new world, a soldier into the role of officer, and the reader into scientific and social speculation. The initiation plot proves very helpful. Haldeman uses it to introduce his speculation and his characters, and to develop his themes.

Because William Mandella is forever an initiate, he is forever learning. As the narrator, he records what he learns as he learns it, in his own conversational way. The result for the reader is concise, clear explanations of the speculations that make this work science fiction and that are incorporated into the plot. That awkward "expository lump" is formed when the plot stops while the author presents information that will initiate his readers into the world he has posited. By making the protagonist, in this case also the narrator, share the struggles of the initiate, the plot need not halt, and the explanations can also be couched in terms that further permit it to blend into the fiction. As William Mandella learns about collapsar jumps, so do we. As he is introduced to the reality of an earth entirely homosexual, we are introduced to its possibilities. As we share the narrator's experiences with his brave new world, we find ourselves a part of it too and accept it as objective reality for the duration.

Initiation rites test character: each time Mandella is introduced to a new experience, his performance reveals his character. The first time Mandella fights the Taurans, his moral code (which is pacifist) and the efficiency of the army's psychological conditioning (which overrides his pacifism with bloodthirsty, if inaccurate, thoughts) are tested. The results: Mandella is an efficient warrior sickened by his artificially induced bloodlust. The army's attempt to make him a soldier in general is in part successful, but his own attempt to be himself in particular is not completely futile. The test reveals in Mandella's character a war between his soldiering and his individual integrity and shows his individual strength in the face of depersonalizing experiences. Further initiations and further tests reveal further elements of Mandella's character until, by the end of the novel, Haldeman has built a character both generalized as a military Everyman and individualized as William Mandella.

The Forever War's initiation plot economically develops Haldeman's theme of future shock. In the second section of the novel, Mandella quotes his commodore's lecture on the subject:

> Back in the seventies, some people felt that technological progress was so rapid that people, normal people, couldn't cope with it; that they wouldn't have time to get used to the present before the future was upon them. A man named Toffler coined the term *future shock* to describe this situation (Section 5, "Sergeant Mandella," *FW*).

This is William Mandella's situation as he is introduced into one new society after another, and it is our problem as we are presented with one new speculation after another. Mandella copes with the massive changes he meets because he tries to understand them intellectually, looks for logical explanations of how things have come to be, tries to understand just how they are; he also has a touchstone, Marygay. "Marygay and I were each other's only link to real life, the Earth of the 1980's" ("Lieutenant Mandella," *FW*). He copes, though the new times are not "real life," not his home.

The Forever War initiates us into various futures, and we too must cope with future shock. This is quite a common affliction among science-fiction readers. Its symptoms include confusion about terms and puzzlement over customs, social order, inventions, and new techniques, all of which bear on the reader's understanding of plot and character and many of which need explanation if we are to cope with our future shock. Haldeman uses plot and character, initiation and initiate to help us cope. We cope because we witness Mandella's logical explanations and try to understand the speculation intellectually and because we also have two touchstones, William Mandella and the army. Mandella is from our own near future: he is our link to much of the language, routine, and philosophy that we know and understand.

The Two Forever Wars

It is no accident that the future army that Haldeman posits, and which helps us survive our future shock, has so close a resemblance to our own. *The Forever War* teaches us about how we have handled the historically recent past by showing its parallels in the future. It is a science-fiction novel about Vietnam and it is also one which is, to an extent, autobiographical.

"You have the desire to impose your ideas on other people, but not your will" (sec. 1, "Major Mandella," *FW*). This is a description of William Mandella, but it might also serve to describe Joe Haldeman. Mandella is not Haldeman, only a persona, but there are some resemblances. Mandella's character, which offers a reason for Haldeman's need and motive for writing, shows one point of similarity between Mandella and Haldeman. The others are more generalized and largely concern war: like Haldeman, Mandella was a student with a physics degree when he was drafted into a war he could not justify; like Haldeman, he was seriously injured; like Haldeman, he learned the lessons of war; and like Haldeman, he returned to a much-altered civilian life.

The novel operates on a "metaphorical level as a discussion of Vietnam, war and its effect on American society, with special reference to the situation of returned veterans (write what you know)" (letter, June 13, 1978). *The Forever War* has a number of parallels to Vietnam. The future army is riddled with SNAFUs, e.g., inadequately training and outfitting soldiers for the climates in which they will fight. The soldiers are ordered to kill innocents, not women and children as in Vietnam, but teddy bear aliens, because they *might* be dangerous, though no effort is made to communicate and find out whether there is actual danger beyond the assumption. The army does its best to depersonalize its soldiers, turning them into automated killing machines. And many of the machines are crippled. Maiming in war is a recurring event in Haldeman's fiction: here Mandella loses a leg, Marygay an arm, another character has lost everything from the waist down and is a cyborg.

Like those in Vietnam, the soliders in the Forever War are trained only for war and are unable to become part of civilian life when they do return to it. And civilian life has changed and become alien to the returned veterans. As if this weren't enough, the returned veterans are an embarrassment to the civilians. They are reminders of unpleasantness for those who are waiting out the war in blissful ignorance, and later, when the war is over, they are reminders of awful mistakes.

As in the Vietnamese war, lives are merely counters for the army, and personal talent has nothing to do with warfare: it is all computers, probability, and complex impersonal factors.

Wars are won not by a simple series of battles won, but by a complex interrelationship among military victory, economic pressures, logistic maneuvering, access to the enemy's information, political postures . . . . (Sec. 5, "Sergeant Mandella," *FW*).

The lessons Mandella learns from the forever war are the same lessons Haldeman learned from Vietnam. What the female man who welcomes Mandella back from his last mission says about the forever war is what Haldeman says about Vietnam:

The 1,143-year-long war had been begun on false pretenses and only continued because the two races were unable to communicate (Sec. 8, "Major Mandella," *FW*).

The Forever War is not an allegory, however.

32

"In the first part of *The Forever War*, I was trying to do a parallel with the American involvement in Vietnam, and then the story took over, and just went its own way. But oddly enough, a reader in India got in touch with me (at a meeting of S[cience] F[iction] L[eague of] I[owa] S[tudents] in Iowa City) and showed me chapter and verse how the *last half* of the book followed the American involvement. I had written it before we had quit the war, and the whole thing followed in a metaphorical way. Well, he was right, and I was simply drawing on the only war that I have experienced, and so that was my psychological background for the thing and I subconsciously followed it. But I stopped doing it consciously after the first fifty pages or so" (Darrell Schweitzer, "An Interview With Joe Haldeman," *Science Fiction Review*, February 1977, p. 27).

Parallels with *Starship Troopers*

"That was my psychological background for the thing and I subconsciously followed it." This statement about Haldeman's Vietnam sources might also apply to Haldeman's use of *Starship Troopers* (1959) by Robert A. Heinlein, a science-fiction novel he had read three or four times before he had even thought of writing *The Forever War*. There is a striking similarity in situations and an equally striking dissimilarity in attitudes to the military. A reader might think *The Forever War* was a conscious reply to Heinlein's view, a reaction against it. This is not the case.

Was *The Forever War* in any way a response to *Starship Troopers*?
Haldeman: "No. That's interesting . . . . I got seventy pages into it before somebody pointed out that I had stolen plot, all of the characters, all of the hardware from *Starship Troopers*. It hadn't occurred to me" (Schweitzer's interview, as cited above, p. 26).

When I asked Haldeman what in his own writing came from Heinlein, he mentioned "setting up a protagonist who can deal with life not painlessly but reasonably, get through anything" (interview, June 6, 1978). This is a description of William Mandella (and others); it is also a description of the protagonist of *Starship Troopers*.

Nevertheless, *The Forever War* is not *Starship Troopers*, not by a long shot. *Starship Troopers*' protagonist enlists; is a willing, indeed an enthusiastic participant in his nation/world's warfare; and Heinlein's view of society and war is light-years from Haldeman's. In Heinlein's world corporal punishment is lauded, and war is a noble effort with clearly defined good and evil neatly marshaled to opposing sides. This is not the world Haldeman sees now nor is it the one of his novel.

"I have little enough sympathy for the attitude expressed in *Starship Troopers*, and I'm not sure Heinlein would be a hundred percent sympathetic with it either. Heinlein expressed a reasonable way to fight a certain kind of war with a certain kind of population backing it, and I did the same sort of thing. I think that my type of population is closer to what I see as a 1970's reality, and his is closer to what he sees as a 1940's reality. I don't think that the population of today would support the army going out for a *Starship Troopers* kind of war, not without a lot of conditioning" (Schweitzer's interview, as cited above, p. 26).

Speculating

Haldeman takes care that his speculations about future warfare are plausible extrapolations from our present society, but he is not attempting to predict the actual future. There are those who do attempt to predict the future, "futurists" they call themselves, but they believe that they deal in the realm of non-fiction. Science fiction does not claim to offer winning predictions of our single actual future: it does sometimes warn us of the possible consequences of our present mode of living or suggest to us the implications of what we now do. To the extent an author has read the present well, his fiction will seem plausible: we will see something of our mundane lives reflected in his future world.

Sometimes Haldeman, when he shows us a future of military clones, is warning us of the dehumanizing process now going on in a conformity-happy present. Certainly he warns us that our recent stance in warfare is a dangerous one and that the attitudes that brought about our involvement in Vietnam could continue to bring us bloodshed and dehumanization. Though he is not predicting that we will necessarily become an entirely homosexual society, he is showing us that a world that conforms to one rigid set of sexual stereotypes is no utopia.

Appraisal

The Forever War deserves its reputation as a bold innovation in science fiction. It looks at traditional props of science fiction—bug-eyed monsters, inter-galactic warfare, and the soldier initiate—in new ways. The bug-eyed monsters suffer, panic, learn, and forgive misunderstandings. The warfare is harsh, unnecessary, and both psychically and physically damaging. The soldier is more than a *tabula rasa* on which adventures and polemics are imprinted: he is a sexual, ethical, and emotional determiner of plot direction. He is a character.

The most notable of the hard science-fiction writers (I am thinking particularly of Arthur C. Clarke and Isaac Asimov) expend most of their energies upon the science, not upon character, not upon style. Haldeman's science is as thoroughly developed and as accurate as Asimov's, for instance, but for Haldeman the science is only a part of the world he creates and attention to style and character become important contributions to the whole.

Mandella may seem eccentric to some of his fellow characters in the future army of *The Forever War*, but to his post-Vietnam readers, he is representative of the armies of our recent past. He is accessible to us though he lives in an inaccessible world.

One of the great strengths of *The Forever War* is its responsible morality. Haldeman is very careful to make his protagonist a moral man who abhors violence and injustice, even though he is part of an amoral universe. Haldeman makes a point of avoiding sexual stereotyping (though we might find it in the obligatory sexual rotation of women and in the flighty homosexual men). He sees Marygay Potter as a protagonist equally as important as Mandella; because Mandella, not Potter, is the viewpoint character, she is not so central a figure to the novel, but she is the central character in Mandella's life.

Haldeman also took considerable care to select a style that would best show us the objective reality of his vision. That style is not one strikingly new to science fiction. The Hemingway plain style and the sequence of motion and fact are not more uncommon to science fiction than they are to mainstream fiction, though Haldeman uses them here in an uncommonly controlled way. Though the tools are borrowed, he has nevertheless crafted a well-executed piece of fiction with them. A great artist would invent new tools to do new things, and Haldeman has not done that nor has he pretended to. He has adapted the tools of Hemingway to a new sort of hero and a new sort of war: in these ways he makes the best use of his precursors.

V

MINDBRIDGE

Mindbridge represents change for Haldeman in a number of ways. There is little autobiography beyond a certain parallel between the protagonist's relationship with his strong and supportive partner and Haldeman's with his wife. Haldeman sees another instance that is autobiographical. "The scene of sexual intercourse under telepathy: the idea that it would be wonderfully cuddly-pornographic for some people and a disastrous invasion of privacy for others. (I've been both people myself, which I think is what it's about)" (letter, April 25, 1979). Haldeman is always present in some way in his protagonists, it seems.

The subject of this novel is not war—that nightmare has been controlled by the "scriptotherapy" (to borrow Barth's term in *End of the Road*) of the first two novels. There is less violence than previously and less hard science. In fact, psychic communication, the basic premise of the novel, is something Haldeman believes is without scientific basis and nonexistent: he used it because it suited his purposes. The female protagonist is much stronger than the one in *The Forever War*, and the documentary style that he used sparingly in the first two novels is now a major aspect of this work.

Haldeman compresses Dos Passos' panoramic documentary collage to paint his futuristic background. This is a different future from that of *The Forever War*, one in which matter transmission, not collapsar jumps, has made interstellar exploration and colonization, not interstellar war, feasible. Beyond this development, the future of *Mindbridge* seems a technologically snappy extension of our present, without the political, social, or ecological upheaval assumed in *The Forever War's* postulations.

In this future live Jacque LeFavre and Carol Wachal, Tamers of newly explored planets, who, along with their team, discover an unprepossessing pudding of a creature that nevertheless causes a psychic link between the people touching it. This mindbridge, found on an anomalous planet, makes possible mindreading, the most direct, most powerful, and most dangerous form of communication. It also facilitates, as LeFavre and his fellow human beings learn from the deadly calm alien L'vrai, humanity's first steps away from millions of unconnecting and uncommunicating atoms to a single group identity with individuals closely connected by instananeous and perfect communication.

Its Writing and Publishing

The Forever War had been a smash, and this made Haldeman's future a matter for speculation among science-fiction fandom. Would the next science-fiction novel be just like the first one? Would it be as good? Haldeman, a fan himself, was aware of this speculation, and it might have caused him some anxiety in his writing, but for three things that helped insure him against the

36

freeze that might occur in trying to beat his own record. First, he already had a plan for the next novel; he is never without writing projects that will extend into the next five years. Second, he had his strict daily writing routine to make writing an inevitable process. Third, he had the continued confident support of his wife and his closest friends in fandom. While fandom exerts pressure by its expectations, these expectations, when combined with the personal warmth fandom can offer, can be quite supportive.

Mindbridge took time to write (he began it in September, 1974, and finished it in November, 1975), but it was a book he enjoyed writing. "I knew what to do every time I was sitting down at the typewriter . . . . I had a lot of fun with that book. [I'd] really get up from the typewriter exhilarated" (interview, June 6, 1978).

Teaching took up much of the time he would have spent with his own writing. Also taking time from *Mindbridge* were his obligations for books he had contracted to do. This was the point in Haldeman's career, just after success had burgeoned, when he was offered contracts that he felt he must accept in order to win financial security. The contracts guaranteed this, but at the same time they demanded writing to orders that may not have suited his inclinations. Haldeman, before he was done, had contracted to write two adventure novels of Attar the Merman, two Star Trek novels, and a non-fiction work on space colonization, as well as *Mindbridge*, the one contract on which he had artistic freedom. Only in 1979, five years later, did he completely finish these obligations. The contracts caused him tension and frustration, but they also helped make him financially independent so he could not entirely resent or regret them.

Haldeman did much planning for *Mindbridge*. "I made up a cardfile— I realized it was going to be a very complicated book—and I tried to get a sequence of events and biographies of characters and such" (interview, June 6, 1978). He also made up an outline, what he describes as "a condensed story line" (interview, November 1, 1977), which St. Martin's Press finally accepted in May, 1975. How closely did he follow these particular plans? The cardfile —"I abandoned it" (interview, June 6, 1978). And the outline—"the ending is almost exactly what I had planned and nothing in between is what I had thought" (interview, November 1, 1977).

The less structured preparations turned out to be more helpful. He planned to use John Dos Possos' documentary technique "but compress it and boil it down . . . so I took the Dos Passos technique and applied it to only one story—that is, only one main character—and compressed it violently" (from Clifford McMurray's "An Interview with Joe Haldeman," *Thrust: SF in Review*, Fall 1978, p. 19) "I tried it out in a short story first, and it seemed to work so I went ahead and did it" (from the *Thrust* interview, p. 21.). That story was "To Howard Hughes: A Modest Proposal," first published in the November, 1974, *Magazine of Fantasy and Science Fiction*, anthologized in *Study War No More* and *Infinite Dreams*. The exercise proved to him that his technique would work, and off he went on *Mindbridge*.

Reactions

Mindbridge received generally favorable, indeed a few very enthusiastic, reviews. A number of reviews—Gerald Jonas' in *The New York Times Book Review, Kirkus Reviews*, Algis Budrys' in *The Magazine of Fantasy and Science Fiction*, and Dave Samuelson's in *Locus*—suspected the novel of being all flash and no fire, though they admired the flash. *The Times Literary Supplement* found the flashy form "a good hard-boiled way of telling a story about survival ethics," and Spider Robinson, reviewing in *Galaxy*, thought the book "a genuine masterpiece." Two science-fiction critics, Dave Samuelson, and Joe Sanders in *Delap's F and SF Review*, wrote rather lengthy comparissons of *Mindbridge* to *The Forever War*. Though they came to different conclusions (Samuelson felt *The Forever War* was the better book, Sanders preferred *Mindbridge*), both saw similarities between the plots of the two novels. As Sanders summarizes it, "Young hero, incomprehensible enemy, love under threat of imminent separation and death, combat in space, etc." (from Sanders' review of *Mindbridge* in the January 1977, issue of *Delap's F and SF Review*, p. 24). Sanders expresses another characteristic reaction in calling the novel's form "looser than that of *The Forever War*." Certainly the short sections and their numerous forms do give that first impression. Actually, the structure of *Mindbridge* is very tight. The library journals were much fonder of *Mindbridge* than they had been of *The Forever War*—it was cleaner, after all, and the author now had an established reputation.

Because *The Forever War* had been a success and because *Mindbridge* was selling very nicely in hardback, the bidding for paperback rights was lively: Avon won with a sturdy $100,000, the highest ever paid for a science-fiction work at that time (Summer of 1976). Avon took care of its investment by implementing a big advertising campaign, including television spots, full-page advertisements in science fiction magazines, and a cover that doesn't mention science fiction to attract a mainstream audience.

Mindbridge: A Two-Part Structure
Inside and Out

"Life is episodic," but *Mindbridge* is less episodic than the first two novels had been. Instead, it is divided into two parts with, appropriately, a bridge at the center. The first half of the book, incorporating sections 1 through 24, deals with Jacque LeFavre the individual and with the mindbridge. The bridge at the center, sections 25 and 26, deals with Jacque and Carol's duties as breeders of new populations on new planets. The second half, sections 27 through 53, concerns the L'vrai and Jacque LeFavre the public figure. At first glance, the two halves of the novel seem to be at odds with one another, but further examination shows that this is far from the case. The organization forms a complex interrelated structure related to the novel's use of two predominant stylistic techniques: chapters that advance the plot and are written in a vigorous, curt manner from a third-person objective viewpoint, and documents of two sorts: excerpts from LeFavre's autobiography and artifacts of LeFavre's society.

The first half of *Mindbridge* sets up the personality of the protagonist and the attributes of the newly discovered creature. We learn about LeFavre in several ways. The chapters tell us his actions so we learn about his exterior life. They also reveal his thoughts, as they do the thoughts of other characters, so we also learn something of his interior life. The first-person sections show us his thoughts as he records them, so we learn about his interior life paradoxically from a document, a piece of exterior evidence. The other documents give us more exterior information about LeFavre by telling us about the environment in which he lives and by showing us how his organization views him officially. These documents show the individual as he relates and reacts to his more generalized roles as employee and child of his times.

The second half of the novel develops LeFavre's role as expert and empath of the mindbridge, as liaison between man and the L'vrai. The chapters and documents function as they did in the first half, but they are presented in different proportions. In the second half, there is more interior information about the exterior life of LeFavre.

The bridge between the two halves contains one autobiographical section (an interior glimpse) and one document (an exterior one). The subject matter, the breeding of human beings, links the individual (LeFavre's sexual attitudes, his unique genetic composition) to the general (LeFavre's role as breeder, his continuance of a genetic line).

The following chart pinpoints and speedily illustrates the proportions of each sort of story-telling technique in the three major parts of the novel.

	Chapters & chapter-like sections	Auto-biography	Other documents	Total sections
Part I (sections 1-24)	10	1	13	24
Bridge (sections 25 & 26)	0	1	1	2
Part II (sections 27-53)	15	4	8	27
	both interior and exterior	interior	exterior	

The movement then is from a relatively objective view of an individual to a relatively subjective view of a generalized entity. This is also the movement of humanity's evolution in the book. First humankind is a chaotic mix of unconnected and uncommunicative atoms. The mindbridge connects individuals so they can communicate for limited times. Finally the L'vrai show(s) how all sentient beings, human and otherwise, can be totally linked so that the concept of the individual disappears and all act as one. This feat is made possible by opening up the entire interior life of every individual to every other one. Interior becomes exterior.

The story that at first seems to be two unresolved elements, unconnected atoms, is actually carefully connected in such a way that the style and structure illuminate the content and theme. And since Haldeman is not particularly impressed by the possibility of telepathy, we can assume that communication, not telepathy, is the theme. Philosophers and politicians have offered numerous techniques for attaining universal harmony, from love to a common enemy: Haldeman offers open communication. Truly honest communication may be as difficult to attain as Jesus' universal love, but saviors don't seem to offer many solutions. That is what Jacque LeFavre becomes finally. Like Jesus, he proves that there is a life beyond death. In the last autobiographical section of the book, he enters the mind of his great-granddaughter to experience "ecstasy death." There he meets the mind of his wife Carol, dead for 17 years.

Haldeman isn't promising us eternal life in this section, any more than he had promised the future attainment of telepathy. I believe he is telling us that unveiled and unambiguous communication eliminates the misunderstandings and misleading machinations that lead to pain and destruction in every relationship from the most intimate to the most universal. Carol and Jacque have an openly honest relationship—it blossomed when they made love (albeit unsuccessfully) under the influence of the mindbridge. *The Forever War* would never have been fought if humanity and the aliens had attempted direct, unmanipulative communication.

Open communication demands not only honesty but self-knowledge, which is the journey made during the first half of the book. The L'vrai simply gave what the minds they contacted expected—violence. Humanity communicated xenophobia, a direct enough communication, but a destructive one. Humanity had misled itself by fear (true communication from the beginning would eliminate fear) and communicated a feeling it didn't want to possess.

A Novel of Character

Haldeman sees *Mindbridge* as a novel of character. Jacque LeFavre is obviously the central figure, and Haldeman takes much care to develop his character through various documents that reveal his childhood, his relationship with his father, his attitudes toward authority and co-workers: and through his experiences with the mindbridge. Section 19, "Fugue," is the most important example of this. We are witnesses to Carol and Jacque as they try to make love while in contact with the mindbridge. Haldeman shows us Jacque's mental experience as it is filtered through Carol's mind, and Carol's filtered through Jacque's. We learn a great deal about Jacque's attitude toward sex, toward Carol, toward people, and toward life in general in this economical use of two viewpoints filtered through one another and presented simultaneously. The two typographical columns of simultaneous speech that Haldeman sets up are, ideally, meant to be read at the same time, the way that binocular vision combines to resolve a single image.

This scene, as well as others, also teaches us about Carol's character.

40

Though Haldeman saw Marygay Potter as one of the two main characters of *The Forever War*, her character was not so thoroughly developed as is Carol's. Marygay's prime purpose was as a reflective surface to show Mandella's character and as a romantic ideal for him to attain. Though she was represented as an intelligent, sensual, and independent woman, Mandella was the stronger character in every way.

In *Mindbridge*, the female protagonist has been strengthened. Though she is not the central character with whose history we are most concerned, she is an influential one, and a character who is stronger in many ways than the male protagonist. LeFavre is not entirely well balanced: he acts with a quick temper and mixed motives. Carol is more stable, more open socially if not telepathically, more confident in dangerous situations than Jacque, and she serves as his protector when his life is endangered. She is much more than a reflecting surface, though she must serve that purpose as well. She is a prime operator in the world of the novel.

Appraisal

Mindbridge is the best novel of Haldeman's still blossoming career, with the novel *Worlds* still awaiting publication at this writing. *Mindbridge* has convincing science, interesting and original speculation, lively action, and solid characterization. So it is a successful science-fiction novel, more successful than *The Forever War*. The characters of *Mindbridge* combine the individual with the general more than do those of *The Forever War*. Mandella was an Everyman while LeFavre is a more complex amalgam, so he is more intriguing to examine. The speculation is less closely related to previous science-fiction literature, so it seems fresher, and the science, in the form of various charts and explanations, is as lucidly presented as it was in *The Forever War*.

The structure and style of *Mindbridge* lift it to a higher plane than *The Forever War*. Though Haldeman is still adapting the style of another author, he is controlling it and molding it to his own purposes so that it is utterly suitable. The overall structure of the novel, with the two sections connected by a bridge, is beautifully balanced and tightly binds story and theme.

Mindbridge has a few fascinating hints at meta-fiction (fiction about fiction). The autobiography sometimes consists of excerpts from *Peacemaker: The Diaries of Jacque LeFavre*, published by St. Martin's, Haldeman's publisher. There are two imaginary books cited in this future history called Mindbridge: *Mindbridge: A Preliminary Evaluation*, a text on the phenomenon; and *Mindbridge* by Jacque LeFavre (published by St. Martin's). In addition, in section 52, there is an editor's note that calls the *Mindbridge* we have read a collection. All these Mindbridges make boxes within boxes and show us a tantalizing bird's-eye view of the book we are reading. After convincing us thoroughly of the objective reality of his fiction, Haldeman zooms out to a perspective that makes us see his book simultaneously as a history (objective) and as a mind game (subjective): a neat trick. The meta-fiction game and the complex structure never detract from the novel's science-fictional aspects, so it does not become an abstruse intellectual exercise, but remains accessible and enjoyable as a story.

VI

ALL MY SINS REMEMBERED

Joe Haldeman's fourth novel is in many ways a disappointment, relying heavily as it does on the last few pages to tie together three otherwise uneven and rather unrelated episodes. But it is an interesting, entertaining, and even a forward-moving disappointment in which Haldeman confidently employs his own style, shows his continued interest in interior and exterior influences upon character, and makes quite clear for the first time just how black his view of life-as-career is.

The novel is three episodes in the life of Otto McGavin, a spy whose disguises are almost complete transformations of his body and personality. Through hypnosis and plastic surgery, the TBII, McGavin's sinister governmental employer, can almost completely alter McGavin's thinking and appearance. In each episode, McGavin confronts violence and megalomania in his antagonists and in his own organization. The episodes are distant from one another chronologically, but there are interchapters before and after each episode that attempt to pull them together into an episodic novel about career and disillusionment.

Fits and Starts: the novel's writing and publishing

The writing of *All My Sins Remembered* included long gaps between episodes. It began when Haldeman wrote a story to fit an anthology on "crime in the twenty-first century," which editor Hans Stefan Santessan mentioned at the 1970 Disclave convention.

"Well, I wanted to do a story about aliens, so I figured the exploitation of alien races . . . is certainly a crime that won't be possible until we find alien races to exploit" (letter, July 24, 1979). Soon after the seed was planted, Haldeman mentioned to a friend "the odd practice among the ancestor-worshipping Montagnards, that they considered their (recently) dead ancestors to be active members of the household and consulted them familiarly on day-to-day matters. Wouldn't it be gruesome if they had them pickled or mummified, sitting around the house . . . hmmm . . . .

"Anyhow, that's how 'To Fit the Crime' got written . . . . I wrote the thing in ten days (long days). It occurred to me that there was the nucleus of a book there, a spy thriller, but I didn't do much with the idea. I remember typing up a page or so of notes; the book would begin with Otto's youth, with 'To Fit the Crime' being the penultimate episode" (same letter).

This story was published in the April, 1971, *Galaxy*, but before it came out, Holt, Rinehart, and Winston had accepted the outline for *War Year* and Haldeman turned all his energies to that.

"About a year later . . . Jakobbson [then editor of *Galaxy*] called me and said he'd had so much good response to the McGavin story that he wanted another one. He'd pay me $2000 for 20,000 words. That was more than any other magazine paid at the time. So I did 'The Only War We've Got'...."

"Jake liked the story [after Haldeman has spruced it up with monsters] and offered to buy a third novella for $1000; furthermore he said he'd put all three in a book and Award (their pb imprint) would give me $2500 advance for it.

"Well, I was hard at work on *The Forever War*, and I told Jake I'd do it when I could. It's a good thing I didn't get around to it; the book would have sunk out of sight and I'd be about fifty grand poorer.

"I did continue thinking about it, though, and realized that three spy tales would make a pretty thin book. The last one had to redeem it .... But some years went by before I actually wrote it" (same letter).

About four years passed before Haldeman wrote the last episode and the interchapters. Meanwhile, he had become a major name.

After the years of sporadic work, Haldeman felt the result was disappointing.

"The spy stuff overshadowed what I took to be the main theme. It was well-reviewed, though, and made a large paperback sale and is being printed in about a dozen different countries, so it's evidently not too bad a book.

"I obviously like the last section of the book best; it was written six or seven years after the other two tales. The whole thing was slightly rewritten, though. I blue-pencilled the magazine stories [the first two episodes] and gave them to an Iowa City typist to retype ....

"When I sent the manuscript in, I suggested to Tom Dunne [at St. Martin's] that he bind a razor blade in with the last page, for the convenience of readers who wanted to slash their wrists. He didn't" (same letter).

All My Sins Remembered received mixed reviews, and many recognized Haldeman as something of a master in his field by this time, though they didn't necessarily find this book a masterpiece: the library journals seemed particularly mindful of his credentials. The harshest reviews came from *Kirkus Reviews* (September 15, 1977, p. 1014), which felt that the novel reduced "moral outrage to a trivial, extraneous 'message,' " and from *Analog* (March 1978, pp. 165-166); *Analog's* reviewer was the science-fiction novelist Lester del Rey, who complained that it was a novel "patched together out of the writer's shorter works." Del Rey found this to be a mortal sin: "In all kindness, this is a novel better forgotten." Such an extreme judgment might leave an entertaining novel unread and accuses Haldeman unfairly of forcing unrelated novellas into an unnatural relationship. While we might wish the novellas a tighter coordination, they were all meant to become, together, a novel, almost from the beginning.

Examining the Episodes

"Life is nothing but episodic. There's no continuity to anybody's life. Who do you know who has simply progressed through life? You stumble along and then something good happens, or something bad happens . . . . There are no patterns you can rely on. And sometimes literature imposes patterns that are esthetically pleasing but it doesn't have to" (interview, June 6, 1978). With this view of reality and Haldeman's desire to teach us about reality, it is no wonder that *All My Sins Remembered*, like his earlier novels to greater and lesser extents, is episodic in nature. Because the episodic structure reflects Haldeman's view of the world, it is a strength.

However, it is not so smoothly handled here as it was in *The Forever War*. Both novels had originally been published as a series of separate novellas, and both had been intended to become novels. Only after the first novella had been completed did Haldeman see *All My Sins Remembered* forming, whereas *The Forever War* started growing halfway through this first novella. Further, *The Forever War* had been written with more consistent attention to the major elements of the novel than had *All My Sins Remembered*. Because of these factors, the closer chronological relationship between the episodes and the addition of another continuing character, Marygay Potter, *The Forever War* presents a more closely unified impression.

The major problems of *All My Sins Remembered* center in the episode called "The Only War We've Got." "I've tried to write longhand. It's been a dismal failure. It doesn't look like writing, like the printed word. I wrote the first 80 pages [of "The Only War We've Got"] for a magazine, longhand. I was going at a white heat, writing in Cuban restaurants in Key West. So easy, but terrible when I typed it up.

"The monsters weren't in the original story. Ejlar Jakobsson of *Galaxy* printed the first one, wanted another, made me an offer of one thousand dollars. And he said, 'Hey, this isn't SF. It could happen in South America.' I said, 'You tumbled to it, Jake.' He wanted some monsters" (interview, November 3, 1977).

McGavin's personality overlay in this episode is a thoroughly unpleasant one, that of a sex-mad assassin, well-suited to a violently hostile planet crawling with vicious carnivores and hot-blooded Latins. The characters of this episode are all "macho males" or damsels in distress, hopelessly entangled in stereotypic behavior. Even the politics are stereotypic, redolent of seamy South American upheavals. There are no intriguing new ideas like the alien philosophies of the first and last sections. There is little development of Otto McGavin's own personality, little furthering of understanding about the sinister nature of the TBII or any absorbing career. The prose itself is not sloppy, and the section is "a good read" but, as Haldeman points out, it may as well not be science fiction.

Since Haldeman wrote the first section, "To Fit the Crime," rather early in his career, we might expect it to be weak, but this isn't the case. It is legitimate science fiction rather than transplanted mainstream fiction: without the aliens and their attitudes toward life and death, there would be no story. McGavin's personality overlay doesn't totally obliterate McGavin: we learn how it feels to be submerged inside another personality and gain some insight into McGavin's own personality. And in McGavin's repeated assurances—made in the face of evidence——that the TBII wouldn't throw away the lives of its prime operators, we get some inklings into the nature of the organization.

A comparison of the magazine version of "To Fit the Crime," published in 1971, with the book version, published in 1977, shows that Haldeman had learned a good deal about prose style in the interim and made use of it in revision.

The 1971 version opens:

The pot-bellied, graying man walked down the corridor to the psychiatrist's stateroom, one of two such rooms on the interstellar vessel. He stood in the open door, then tapped lightly to get the man's attention (*Galaxy*, April 1971, p. 4).

The novel, published six years later, begins:

Every direction seems uphill in artificial gravity. Isaac Crowell, Ph.D., paused to get his breath, pushed damp hair back from his forehead, and tapped the door of the psychiatrist's stateroom. It slid open (*AMSR*, sec. 1, "To Fit the Crime").

The second version avoids pushing information ("one of two such rooms . . ."), dives immediately into the experience of being a "pot-bellied, graying man" by showing us how it feels ("Every direction seems uphill," "paused to get his breath, pushed his damp hair back") rather than telling us how the man looks, and is wittier, more distinctive in tone, and more active than the *Galaxy* version published six years earlier.

The third episode, "All My Sins Remembered," was to be published by *Cosmos Magazine*, which folded before the story appeared. It is the best of the three episodes. Its aliens, large beetles with a gift for snide repartee and a reticence for straight answers, are engaging enough for us to care about their fate at the hands of human enemies. Otto McGavin battles with the evil personality in which is submerged, rather than simply becoming that personality as occurs in the second section. The twisted motives of the TBII are developed. The prose style is deft. The plot is more than mainstream fiction with monsters attached and contains events which are evocative of more than a thrill. Obviously sentient, even brilliant creatures are being treated as lab specimens: McGavin, having been transformed into the double of his antagonist, kills the man who looks and acts like "himself."

Here, then, are the three episodes, two of which develop the basic themes of the novel in an episodic way. The structure breaks down in the middle section because Haldeman is less careful with his tools.

When Haldeman collected the three episodes, he added several kinds of unifying interchapters: two interviews, a prologue, and three "redundancy checks." The first interview between McGavin and an evaluating authority of the TBII is a test to see if he'll fit into the organization. He does: "The only problem I see is attitudinal: he's a little too idealistic" (*AMSR*, "Interview: Age 22"), but the TBII plans to fix that. The last interview determines that McGavin's problem is unfixable except by killing him. The prologue is a short preview of the repellent violence McGavin has to look forward to in his career. The redundancy checks, placed between the episodes, are brief biographical summaries of McGavin's career that also reveal his inner conflicts.

45

The interchapters all add to our view of McGavin and his organization, thus emphasizing the common ground of the episodes and the thematic importance of career as life that is the basic thrust of the novel. The last interview, with its shocking last twist, brings us to a sudden realization of the TBII's violation of McGavin's soul. On the one hand, due to the difficulties of the second episode, it might be valid to criticize this as a last ditch effort to clarify, unify, and elevate the novel to something beyond a thriller. On the other hand, such an ending emphasizes the chaos of McGavin's life and the cruel amorality of the powers which control him, factors which had been stressed in two of the three episodes.

"His life was totally futile. He wasn't even really a human being, just a pawn. He doesn't realize it, maybe the reader doesn't realize it, until maybe the last 20 pages" (interview, November 1, 1977).

Reading Otto McGavin

Haldeman uses his episodic structure and his interchapters to form a character study of Otto McGavin, an individual separated from his peers by his struggle to keep his moral will alive and an everyman who represents the many people who risk losing individual identity in their careers, who must struggle to retain any shred of individuality, caught as they are in the totally amoral organizational life. Haldeman shows both interior and exterior influences on the main character and records them from a third-person limited viewpoint using a reliable narrator.

The predominant interior influence on McGavin's life is his stubborn moral will that seems to be part of his basic essence, unreachable through the mind manipulations of the TBII. Two major exterior influences rule in conflict: McGavin's childhood Buddhist training and his later training for the TBII. McGavin's Buddhist training confirms his essential tendency, but the TBII is in such direct conflict that McGavin concludes that the man who was prime operator for the TBII could not truly be Otto McGavin.

Otto McGavin died and was replaced by what I am now, when I'm not someone else

Which is?

Something that walks and talks like Otto McGavin, but is mainly a construct of skills and attitudes installed by continous hypnotic reinforcement by the TBII . . . .

That's nonsense: it's not as if you were brain-wiped.

True, but there are degrees of control, the real Otto McGavin went to temple every evening and tried to follow the Eightfold Path, the construct you call Otto McGavin cheats and steals and kills for a living (*AMSR*, "Interview: Age 45").

This revealing quotation appears in the last interview of the novel. It, like the redundancy checks, is in the form of a transcribed dialog between McGavin

46

and an authority of the TBII. Since these dialogs always occur when McGavin is under hypnosis, they always reveal his subconscious mind. In this way we observe from the outside McGavin's inner life.

Through these windows into his tortured soul, we watch McGavin become more and more upset after each episode, both by the brutality he commits and by that inflicted upon him, including the wrenching away of his identity.

The new arm worked all right? Please go:

Worked better than the old one, my God, the look on the little girl's face

Skip to age 37, please, go:

They tried to use her as a shield, she kept looking at me while she died

Skip to age 37, please, go:

She never even looked at her wound (*AMSR*, "Redundancy Check: Age 39").

Like Hemingway's "A Way You'll Never Be," these interchapters show a man's disintegration under the pressure of his memories (and the scene of a dying horribly, not looking at the wound, is from Haldeman's Vietnam memory bank). As the horrors are dredged up by the demons for biographical recall, McGavin relives them, is oppressed and obsessed by them, and disintegrates. The language shows it, the repetition of image shows it, and the cold insistence of the computer accentuates it.

All the details of McGavin's life, public and private, are recorded by an impersonal reliable narrator who seldom intrudes. McGavin's thoughts come to us through transcribed tapes of the subject under hypnosis. Because of the convention that a person under hypnosis always tells the truth (a convention used with more popularity, if less finesse, in courtroom dramas), we accept these transcripts as objective evidence of McGavin's subconscious.

The three episodes are examples of the sort of job McGavin has been trapped into and show his conflict with that job. Lester del Rey, in his review of *All My Sins Remembered*, makes a perceptive observation:

In each case [each episode], he [McGavin] makes a fool of himself or is made a fool of. He is saved largely by accident from what I consider incompetence in the first story; is saved by the fact that a man is totally different from McGavin's expectations in the second; and is saved (?) by the arrival of another agent in the third. In other words, this Prime Operator, whom we follow for more than twenty years of supposed success in his job, simply goofs off in every case we see (*Analog*, March 1978, pp. 165-166).

The "supposed success" is the TBII's, not McGavin's—he is just a tool. If assignments eat up its Prime Operators and make them look like fools, that simply doesn't matter. McGavin, we come to realize, is a dupe: his morality guarantees him nothing. This lesson, one which Haldeman learned in Vietnam, is a sad part of McGavin's personality, and the episodes teach it. We do not

47

doubt McGavin's experiences or, therefore, his lessons, because they are described in an objective way by the auctorial voice.

Career Man

All My Sins Remembered reveals that the spectres of Vietnam have not yet taken permanent leave of Joe Haldeman: the lessons Vietnam taught him civilian life did not contradict. Otto McGavin's predicament, which illustrates much that the army offered Haldeman, also is a predicament shared by many outside army life. Haldeman describes the theme of *All My Sins Remembered* this way:

> "The idea that Americans, American men especially, see themselves in terms of their professions, almost exclusively. What are you—I'm a teacher, I'm a writer, I'm a computer programmer. Well, that is not all. You're also a husband and lover and father and God knows what else, but you never respond that way. You never say, I'm a husband. It's interesting and I thought it would make an interesting book" (interview, November 1, 1977).

To the government (or to any organization), to society in general, and eventually to an individual, a person *is* his profession, no more. The job can swallow the individual completely and all the hard-earned hours of leisure we end up with may become nothing more than a holding pattern until work begins again.

Science fiction allows the enactment of extremes to make a point: hyperbole impossible in the here and now is possible there. "The point of the book was to be: here's a man who does not exist beyond his profession, literally has no other identity. And when he realizes this, it's fatal to him" (interview, June 6, 1978). Otto's job is to transform 100 per cent of his outer appearance and 90 per cent of his personality into someone else for purposes of espionage. That leaves barely 10 per cent of Otto McGavin, and that 10 per cent has received massive indoctrination and powerful hypnotic suggestion. Of the 10 per cent that remains Otto McGavin is an even smaller proportion that can still be a free agent, unemployed. Literally, McGavin is his career.

Because he is almost completely controlled by his career, McGavin is an apt illustration of several other of Haldeman's lessons. He is a pawn in the TBII's intricate games, and his own fate, whether he lives or dies, is out of his hands. In such a harsh world, McGavin learns to take orders to survive and to concentrate only on living through each dangerous day. And as the TBII turns him more and more into a mechanical tool, McGavin fights more and more to be human and individual. His last futile struggle takes places as he lies

> writhing, naked and hairless, inside the tank of pale blue fluid, chin jerking as he screamed soundlessly, blind eyes staring past the wires that pierced through to the optic nerve (*AMSR*, "Interview: Age 45").

None of us has been subjected to such physical horror in the process of becoming our careers, but all too many of us have been hooked into the machine in other more subtle ways. McGavin's extreme predicament is meant to warn us of the less horrific but still real damage that awaits in a life made over into a job.

There is another spectre of Vietnam which haunts *All My Sins Remembered*: the ugliness of violence, best exemplified by the novel's recurring motif: the little girl who slowly dies, "guts spilling out," as McGavin watches. McGavin the career man is responsible for the brutal death that he, brought up in a pacifist religion, naturally abhors. The individual, that small spark, hates the career man and cannot forget his sins.

Be All My Sins Remembered

While Haldeman was writing the section called "The Only War We've Got," he remembers that "I was over at a friend's house . . . listening to his not so great stereo and definitely inferior album, and I was trying not to listen to it . . . . As a mnemonic to try to get my mind off this terrible music, I was seeing whether I could recite Hamlet's soliloquy. And I got through the soliloquy and the lines following and 'be all my sins remembered' and suddenly the whole book opened up" (interview, November 1, 1977).

Hamlet debates suicide: should he give in to the peace that death offers or should he "fight against a sea of troubles?" For Otto McGavin, brain-wipe would offer the peace that death suggests to Hamlet. He would no longer remember his sins with his entire memory and personality erased. This would be mental death. But McGavin chooses to fight for the right to remember his sins, to remain a moral individual in an amoral organization. This independence is a threat to the organization and forces the TBII into triggering his physical death. McGavin, who acts more than he thinks, has more in common with Laertes than with Hamlet, except for the dilemma upon which McGavin is hooked, as Hamlet was. But it isn't thought that paralyzes McGavin: it is the indoctrination of his career that keeps him from right action.

Speaking in His Own Voice

All My Sins Remembered has a stronger sense of Haldeman's own voice than do his earlier novels. *The Forever War* has strong ties to Hemingway, Crane, and Heinlein; *Mindbridge* owes a debt to Dos Passos: *All My Sins Remembered* suggests most strongly the style of Joe Haldeman.

That style includes humor, sometimes wry, often sardonic, with a fondness for hyperbole and for surprising comparisons and combinations. The alien sometimes known as Balaam's Ass is a prime example of Haldeman's humor. "Balaam's" is quite capable of moving his planet toward and away from its sun by simply considering the action, and his societal role is "keeper of useful sarcasms." Typical of Balaam's (and Haldeman's) humor is the following: when a human archaeologist asks, "What's the square root of the Talmud?" Balaam's replies, "Guilt" (*AMSR*, sec. 3 of "All My Sins Remembered").

Haldeman's prose is smooth, easy, rhythmic, and colloquial without being homespun: it is the style of a sophisticated oral story teller.

He woke up when they loaded him and the doctor machine aboard the shuttle.

He woke up on the ship, twice, to eat.

He woke up when they were unloading the ship, dozens of big insulated containers rolled down the aisle, dormant S'kang [aliens of the Balaam's Ass variety]; humans carried out on stretchers, but they didn't carry him out and he couldn't stay awake.

He woke up for a short time moving from the big ship to a little ship, and he woke up on earth (*AMSR*, sec. 8, "All My Sins Remembered").

The repetition sets up a rhythmic flow and puts the passage in the form of oral story-telling. The vocabulary is consistently the most straightforward, accurate and conversational possible. Not "awakened" but "woke up," the phrase more commonly used in speech. Not "sleeping" but "dormant" to describe the hibernating S'kang. Not "huge" or "tremendous" but simply, accurately, directly, "big" containers. Not "did not" or "could not" but "didn't" and "couldn't," the more colloquial choices. The punctuation is added in places we might not expect to see it, showing us how to speak the lines: "He woke up on the ship, [pause] twice, [pause] to eat."

The presence of a moral center in an amoral universe is a consistent characteristic of Haldeman's plot development. Here there are two, McGavin of the Eightfold Path, and the S'kang.

The only really important things were slowing down at the proper time, rebirth, and tending the flowers properly (*AMSR*, sec. I, "All My Sins Remembered").

The S'kang live without rancor or manipulation, harmonious with natural rhythms, separate from organizational life. Or, as the TBII describes this way of life when describing the non-professional side of McGavin, this is "the selfish pursuit of internal peace and harmony" (*AMSR*, "Interview: Age 45").

A characteristic of Haldeman's style, a very welcome one in science fiction, is his smooth and entertaining exposition of information using a variety of techniques. He may present documents of the world he is building, the technique he used extensively in *Mindbridge*, through the redundancy checks. He may describe a situation that, while it advances the plot, also allows a natural revelation of needed information. For instance, because McGavin cannot remember his hypno-conditioning when he is not hypnotized (we know this because it is revealed in a redundancy check), someone must explain it to him.

Haldeman also uses point of view as a tool for disseminating information. By beginning each episode in the third-person, omniscient viewpoint, he can observe the commonplaces of the new world. As we become more familiar with the setting, he shifts gears to the third-person, limited narrative, so we become personally involved with the main character, while remaining under the auspices of a reliable narrator.

Appraisal

All My Sins Remembered is not of the same caliber as *The Forever War* and *Mindbridge*. The three episodes are not tightly coherent, and the second episode is disappointing. The novel did not seem to grip Haldeman very strongly in the making—he had a hard time gettting to it in the midst of other more interesting projects—though this theme was something about which he feels strongly. The weak grip shows. But the novel still entertains, and we see in it Haldeman's own style more strongly and confidently than in the earlier novels. It is a science-fiction novel still worth reading: fast-paced, witty, with something important to say.

VII

INFINITE DREAMS

Joe Haldeman's one collection of short stories demonstrates his performance in a form that to a great extent disallows his characteristic episodic structure. The traditionally tight order of a short story contradicts Haldeman's view of an essentially chaotic universe. This may be the reason why Haldeman feels more sure of his longer works and often writes his short stories for secondary motives. Many of his short stories are written to fit a narrow set of predetermined rules: to try out a technique or character for a novella or novel, or to satisfy editorial requirements. Such stories are intellectual games in which Haldeman doesn't always have a great deal at stake. When he writes a novel, he exposes his emotional and moral life enough to raise the stakes. Though Haldeman doesn't play a high-risk game in most of his short stories, they are still fun to read, he still plays skillfully, and once in a while he goes for broke. When his stories are particularly successful, they combine character study and strong moral stance with some of his most skillful writing.

Because Haldeman has many tricks to work out, because he likes to publish as frequently as possible (this is how he earns a living), and because it makes him nervous not to produce, he has quite a large bibliography of short fiction. The thirteen stories he gathered for *Infinite Dreams* represent a certain selection process.

Haldeman explains that the process "wasn't a selection in a positive sense, it was more a casting out" (interview, August 5, 1979). First, he eliminated stories that were parts of novels: "Hero," "We Are Very Happy Here," and "End Game" became *The Forever War*; "To Fit the Crime" and "The Only War We've Got" went into *All My Sins Remembered*. "Out of Phase" and "Power Complex" were eliminated because Haldeman may yet combine and add to them for a novel. "Then I cast out things that weren't very good, like 'Two Men and a Rock,' a strange thing I had in a Roger Elwood collection ["John's Other Life"] and a couple of others," like the short plays "The Moon and Marcek" and "The Devil His Due" (same interview). Whether the technique was positive or negative in approach, the result is a pleasing variety of stories that shows Haldeman's versatility. He writes whimsy, satire, and serious fiction, hard science fiction, and fantasy.

The collection has several common motifs. The Washington, D.C. area keeps recurring as the locale for stories, and mathematicians appear in five of them. Less trivial recurrences include crippling and maiming, war, war's preludes and after-effects, the relentless inevitability of fate, and the importance of remaining moral in an amoral and chaotic universe. All these motifs have some sort of autobiographical origin. Though the individual stories are not always charged with high seriousness, the kinds of motifs that repeat themselves in the short pieces confirm what is important in the novels and to Joe Haldeman.

Light-hearted Stories

When Haldeman gives advice to struggling new science-fiction writers, he always suggests humorous science fiction. There is a dearth of funny science fiction but a constant market for it. Two of the stories in the collection, "The Mazel Tov Revolution" and "All the Universe in a Mason Jar," are written for laughs. "The Mazel Tov Revolution" involves very complicated financial finagling by an archetypically Jewish entrepreneur, which is to say that he speaks in Yiddish dialect, not that Haldeman is anti-Semitic. The story, written in the first person, is fast-paced, full of action, and machinations: it never goes beneath the surface of the politics and economics that structure the running of the plot. The chief charm, besides the chatty style and clever use of Yiddish hyperbole and understatement, lies in the fact that the story shows two nobodies who outsmart the ultimate multi-national corporation. "All the Universe in a Mason Jar" is a local color story about moonshine in Florida, embellished with a retired mathematics professor, an alien, and his spaceship, which introduce familiar science-fiction elements. The incongruity of a saurian monster and a Florida moonshiner makes a successful entertainment.

Try-outs

Haldeman says his *metier* is the science-fiction novel, not the short story: often, in fact, the short stories are trial runs to test out techniques or characters he hopes to use in a novel. Or, once finished, some stories may suggest possibilities for a novel. Sometimes they don't point toward a novel at all, but represent a bit of pure research. *Infinite Dreams* contains examples of each sort of short story: the trial run, the suggestion, and pure research.

"To Howard Hughes: A Modest Proposal" is a trial run for *Mindbridge*. As he explains in the introduction to the story, Haldeman wanted to see if he could adapt Dos Passos' collage technique to a science-fiction novel. He knew it could be done, since John Brunner had done it in *Stand on Zanzibar* (1968) and *The Sheep Look Up* (1972). The question was if *he* could, and if he could do it in the boiled-down way he had in mind, limiting the scope to only a few characters instead of following many, as John Dos Passos and John Brunner had done. He wrote "To Howard Hughes" to find out.

Within a twenty-two page short story are twenty-four very short, nervous sections, usually dated, sometimes consisting of a document, a progress report, or quote from "the 2020 edition of Encyclopaedia Britannica." It is a collage of sorts, though it doesn't tell us a great deal of the world surrounding the plot (the world is our present one, the time in 1975, and it is narrowed down to trace only one chain of events). "This story was the test case, and I liked it, so I used the techniques for *Mindbridge*, which I think is my best novel, so far" (introduction to "To Howard Hughes: A Modest Proposal," *ID*). Having made the trial run, Haldeman went on to use the technique to trace not only several chains of events but also the central character in *Mindbridge*. The application was successful.

"Tricentennial" is a suggestion. It began inauspiciously—written to fit a cover illustration by Rick Sternbach for *Analog*. "Though it is one of my favorites, I've never done a story that was so thoroughly written to order" (introduction to "Tricentennial," *ID*). But the result was a short story spanning long centuries and employing the perspective of the wrong end of a telescope to show what might happen to an earth contemptuous of learning (contempt earns oblivion) and to people who fight against ignorance (they may have the chance to start over). The writing in "Tricentennial" is very strong, particularly the epilogue that uses Haldeman's colloquial style in a stately and poetic way:

America itself was a little the worse for wear, this three thousandth anniversary. The seas that lapped its shores were heavy with crimson crust of anaerobic life; the mighty cities had fallen and their remains nearly ground away by the never-ceasing sand-storms (*ID*, "Tricentennial").

He sets up repetitions. rhythmic phrasing, and inverted word order within the basic framework of plain and conversational language.

The character of Abigail Beamis, old enough to be womanly without necessarily being sexual and active enough to be a main character, was too interesting to drop completely when the story ended. "She does foreshadow the major among equals in *Stars* [the second book of the trilogy now in the works]" (interview, August 5, 1979). Abigail Beamis suggested to Haldeman the possibilities of using an older woman, not Beamis but someone rather like her, as a viewpoint character.

"26 Days, On Earth" was more like pure research (or the casting out of a minor demon). The research hypothesis was "can I write an SF story in the manner of the twenty-two-year-old James Boswell?" The question for the writer-as-exorcist was "How can I shake the style of Boswell's *London Journal*?" By answering the second question—write a story—the first question was answered affirmatively.

Destination Zero

Irresistible and negative fate motivates three of the stories: "Counterpoint," "Anniversary Project," and "Armaja Daz." We do not see this concept in blatant form in Haldeman's novels, though it is usually present in some ways. In each of the three stories, a life is predetermined, and not for the best. The individual cannot control his destiny and good works change nothing: destiny is a trap. In "Counterpoint" two children, born of the same father at the same moment to different mothers, are traced through their widely diverging lives to their simultaneous deaths. Wealth, brilliance, and love make no difference in determining their life spans. That has been predetermined.

In "Anniversary Project" a woman who briefly visits the far distant future returns to the present aware of everything that will happen to her. Seeing each moment of her future gives it the inevitability of predetermination, takes away the orderliness of sequential time, and constantly keeps before her all the tortures to which she has to look forward.

"Armaja Das" is no more cheery—here destiny is in the form of a gypsy curse that cannot be avoided, even by the unbeliever. It sets up a chain reaction that turns civilization into rubble. "Armaja Das" was written to order and, after some research on gypsy lore, "it was child's play to toss together gypsy curses, computer science, and minority assimilation into an 'ancient horror in modern guise' " (introduction to "Armaja Das," *ID*). The atmosphere is quite disturbing for a piece of child's play: the empathetic computer that dies to save a man and the carnage its kindness causes make the story more haunting than its seemingly casual birth would suggest.

War Stories

The man who writes novels about war has also written many short stories on the subject. War was the single most influential and devastating thing to happen to Haldeman, an experience that remains even now in his mind, though writing and time have diminished much of the pain. Haldeman includes in *Infinite Dreams* three stories which center on war. "To Howard Hughes: A Modest Proposal" deals with threats of war, "The Private War of Private Jacob" with war itself, and "A Mind of His Own" with its after-effects.

"To Howard Hughes" suggests, in the form of an extrapolated example, that the way to implement disarmament successfully is for an outsider, who would have to be fabulously rich, to threaten atomic retaliation upon any government unwilling to cooperate. Like Swift's "A Modest Proposal," it is not meant to be a practical solution to a problem but to show readers how cruel humanity has been in its past attempts to solve its difficulties. In light of recent fears that people will indeed use nuclear weaponry for blackmail and recent revelations that private production of such bombs is quite possible, the story seems more prophetic than hyperbolic. It does show us how enmeshed such a horrific weapon has become in modern society—here the only way to eliminate it from the common catalog of warfare is to use it; the alternative to war is terrorism.

"The Private War of Private Jacob" is extremely short, a one-idea, one-gimmick story, but done with a powerful image. To love war one must be inhuman, so Haldeman shows soldiers led into war by happy robots. The story's central image of the sergeant laughing while shells burst and men die around him is a strong one; the notion that he or someone like him will always be there is stronger still.

"A Mind of His Own" is, as Haldeman reveals in his introduction to the story, the most autobiographical of the war stories in the collection. The protagonist Shays' injuries are extremes of the author's own, and his forbidding self-pity a disease Haldeman might have fallen victim to, a disease Haldeman watched take its course in a friend. War is not over when the treaties are signed and the fighting has stopped. Leonard Shays' mental and physical anguish are direct effects of war, and they will last him his lifetime.

"I had a friend who was suddenly and severely disabled, and he reacted in a human way, sliding into bitterness . . . driving away his family, then his friends, and then one day I left him too, in spite of knowing how he felt. Exit plaster saint" (introduction to "A Mind of His Own," *ID*). For Haldeman, who sees the world at large as amoral and formless, a strict moral code is the individual's salvation: it is *his* salvation. And the obligations of friendship are an important part of that code. Finding himself unable to meet his own standards (no matter how self-destructive and unreasonable it would have been to do so) diminished Haldeman's confidence in his spirit. As he indicates in the introduction to the story, "A Mind of His Own" was meant to put the demon of his failure to rest. This Haldeman did by turning himself into his friend, thus sharing that friend's suffering; by showing how anyone would have left eventually, he justified his own leaving as a sane and reasonable act.

Traps

"A Mind of His Own" contains the recurring motif of crippling and maiming. Crippling is an outward sign of the damage that war inflicts upon the individual, but Haldeman uses versions and degrees of such crippling in other stories as well, especially in "Juryrigged" and "26 Days, On Earth." Physical disability traps the individual in the cell of his own body and makes him helpless in the face of attacks from outside: it violates his integrity. The protagonist of "Juryrigged" is powerless against the demands of his government or even of any individual who wants to use him. Jonathon Wu in "26 Days" can't defend himself against the bigoted attacks of small-minded people because his low-gravity, lunar muscles and bones carry too little weight on Earth.

Crippling mechanizes a person's movement, makes him rely upon mechanical devices, alienates him from the common run of mankind—he is unwillingly robbed of some of his humanity. The government that literally cripples L. Henry Kennem in "Juryrigged" dehumanizes him by turning him into a computer unit to help run his city. The government, in demanding complete control of Kennem's mind, robs him of a great portion of his humanity as surely as Otto McGavin's career as a spy dehumanized him in *All My Sins Remembered* and William Mandella's work was a soldier made him dream of being a machine in *The Forever War*.

In Haldeman's fiction, physical crippling may be an outward sign of inner limitations as well. Leonard Shays is more thoroughly crippled by his self-pity, anger, and refusal to cope than he is by his physical injuries. Jonathon Wu's arrogant adolescent assumption of superiority limits him more than the braces that support his wobbly limbs.

Summer's Lease

Haldeman says in his introduction to "Summer's Lease" that is is a story about scientific method, and so it is, in part. This story, written at ease and to an editor's specifications, is the best of the collection. Its characterization, landscape, style, and theme combine economically to create a vivid and moving piece of fiction. The protagonist, Lars Martin, stands as a strong individual whose integrity and love for knowledge single him out as a representative of both the value and the unpopularity of wisdom. The world in which

Martin lives is a forgotten Earth colony, whose meteorological violence Haldeman carefully constructs so that it is believable and a vital element of the plot. The writing combines Haldeman's characteristically lucid setting forth of character, event, and theory with Biblical, metrical, and rhymed excerpts from the society's *Godbuk*, both a history and a myth. In choosing a document that should be the central work of the society and therefore its best representative, and that at the same time makes a moving contrast to the rest of the narrative, Haldeman gives this world conviction and reality in the reader's mind.

"Summer's Lease" is indeed about scientific method. Martin uses it slowly, carefully, thoughtfully, to discover the origins of his people and thereby determine how they might be spared the cyclical scourge of utterly destructive storms. Scientific method works, so eventually Martin knows enough of how his society started to begin working out a way to save it. Society finds him, with his knowledge and his offer for salvation, at best humorous and at worst a meddling nuisance. His work is ignored and he is manipulated, through an appeal to his kindness and his love for his people, into ignoring it too. The story honors the scientific method and the progress it makes possible, but it also condemns most of humanity for its cruel determination to remain ignorant. With almost no violence, in an essentially pastoral setting, this short story is Haldeman's most cynical. Hawthorne wrote of scientists violating men's souls to gain knowledge. Here people do the same to remain ignorant.

Appraisal

Infinite Dreams is a fair representation of Haldeman's short story career. He reveals his versatility, never bores, and occasionally shows great strength. His weaknesses are a certain looseness of organization, and, as a part of this looseness, a tendency to cover too much—too many characters, too many plots or plot fragments—at once. The stories often feel like stunted novels. "Summer's Lease," concentrating on one problem and one man while suggesting much more, is an exception. "Armaja Das" concentrates on one line of action and the evocation of one mood, following Poe's idea of unity in short stories: it too has integrity as a short story. "Tricentennial" is beautifully written, with the memorable Abigail Beamis and fascinating speculation, but it leaves much out that could be said: its episodes imply more story than Haldeman supplies, as if it were a moving outline of an invisible novel.

VIII

ANNOTATED PRIMARY BIBLIOGRAPHY
OF THE FICTION

Below is a list, in alphabetical order, of Joe Haldeman's novels, his anthology of his own short stories, and the anthologies of short stories he has edited. Each entry is accompanied by brief remarks designed to serve as simple reminders of the book's content. The major books are discussed more thoroughly in the body of the guide in the appropriately titled chapters.

1. *All My Sins Remembered.* New York: St. Martin's, 1977 (novel). Otto McGavin is an agent for interstellar espionage agency, the TBII. Through hypnosis and plastic surgery, he is transformed into an entity that is 90 per cent the person he impersonates and only 10 per cent himself. This makes him a very effective spy, but the violence and amorality of his career and his agency disgust him. Two of the three novellas which are the bulk of this novel were published in *Galaxy*.

2. *Attar's Revenge.* New York: Pocket Books, 1975 (novel). One of two adventure novels written under the pseudonym Robert Graham. Attar is a man with surgically implanted gills who, with elaborate weapons, practices violent espionage in the name of ecology.

3. *Cosmic Laughter: Science Fiction for the Fun of It.* New York: Holt, Rinehart and Winston, 1974 (anthology). Haldeman edited this collection of humorous science fiction. Only one of the nine selections, "I of Newton," is by him, but he did contribute a short introduction.

4. *The Forever War.* New York: St. Martin's, 1974 (novel). William Mandella and Marygay Potter are soldiers and lovers engaged in a seemingly endless war between humanity and alien beings. The war is patterned after the American war in Vietnam. Four sections of the novel previously appeared in *Analog*.

5. *Infinite Dreams.* New York: St. Martin's, 1978 (anthology). This collection contains thirteen of Haldeman's own short stories, all of which had been published elsewhere. He added personal and informative notes to accompany each story and an equally helpful afterword. The stories are:

"Counterpoint" (1972): the fortunes of two men, born at the same moment to different mothers, though they share the same father, are traced to their simultaneous deaths under vastly different circumstances.
"Anniversary Project" (1974): a man and a woman are transported from 1951 America to a future one million years away.
"The Mazel Tov Revolution" (1974): two men with a scheme attempt to break the hold of the ultimate monopoly by setting up a colony outside its inter-planetary hold.
"To Howard Hughes: A Modest Proposal" (1974): a fabulously rich man devises a way to take nuclear disarmament into his own hands.

The style, a compression of Dos Passos' collage technique, is of special interest.

"A Mind of His Own" (1974): a crippled veteran of a future war refuses therapy or fights off mind control.

"All the Universe in a Mason Jar" (1977): a saurian visitor from another world discovers Florida culture.

"The Private War of Private Jacob" (1974): a constantly smiling and almost indestructible sergeant leads his men into war.

"A Time to Live (1977): the quirks of relativity give a man the chance to live out his life twice, and do it rather better the second time.

"Juryrigged" (1974): jury duty in this future means that the citizen becomes a computer component for a year, helping run his city; not a bad job unless a madman happens to be there too.

"Summer's Lease," previously published as "Truth to Tell" (1974): a man on a planet subject to devastating storms seeks to discover how his people can survive them without losing most of their possessions and many of their lives.

"26 Days, On Earth" (1972): a young man from the moon keeps a diary of his experiences, gaining an education on a rather hostile Earth.

"Armaja Das" (1976): a gypsy curse is visited upon a man who thought he had left his heritage far behind him.

"Tricentennial" (1976): against the isolationist and anti-intellectual political wishes of Earth, a group of scientists heads out on a slow ship to the stars. This story won a Hugo.

6. *Mindbridge*. New York: St. Martin's, 1976 (novel). The history of Jacque LeFavre as he discovers a blob that makes mind-reading possible and a race of beings so integrated in mind that they have no individual identity.

7. *Planet of Judgment*. New York: Bantam, 1977 (novel). One of Haldeman's two Star Trek novels. Interesting to see how he works with the standardized characters, but otherwise minor.

8. *Study War No More*. New York: St. Martin's, 1977 (anthology). Haldeman compiled this collection of ten science-fiction stories that offer alternatives, though not always improvements, to war. He includes his own story, "To Howard Hughes: A Modest Proposal" (see *Infinite Dreams*) as well as short notes accompanying each of the ten stories and a very strong introduction.

9. *War of Nerves*. New York: Bantam, 1975 (novel). The second of Haldeman's adventure novels about Attar the merman. See *Attar's Revenge*.

10. *World Without End*. New York: Bantam, 1979 (novel). The second of Haldeman's Star Trek novels. See *Planet of Judgment*.

11. *War Year*. New York: Holt, Rinehart and Winston, 1972 (novel). Haldeman's first novel, a mainstream work describing a young man's year of combat experience in Vietnam.

War Year. New York: Pocket Books, 1977 (novel). The Holt edition contains the ending that Haldeman's editors requested. This paperback contains Haldeman's original and preferred ending.

IX

ANNOTATED PRIMARY BIBLIOGRAPHY
OF THE NON-FICTION

"Great SF About Artichokes and Other Story Ideas." *Algol*, Summer-Fall 1978, pp. 21-22; Haldeman answers the popular question "Where do you get your crazy ideas?" with "I think all of them came out of nowhere." More helpfully, he goes on to discuss the importance of accurate scientific content and other factual and mechanical detail in convincing both reader and author to believe in a story's reality.

Introduction to *Double Star* by Robert Heinlein. Boston: Gregg, 1978, pp. v-xvi. After announcing his own prejudices—he is bored by most science-fiction criticism, he dislikes politics (*Double Star* is a political novel), and he thinks Heinlein is "the best science-fiction author"—Haldeman explains why, in terms of four functions borrowed from Stephen Becker (a work of art must entertain, educate, edify, and impress), *Double Star* is a great success.

"My Brother, the Writer." *Omni*, May 1979, pp. 30 and 138. Haldeman writes about his brother, Jack C. Haldeman II, who also writes science fiction.

"The Surprising World Called Mercury." *Closeup: New Worlds*. Ed. Ben Bova with Trudy E. Bell. New York: St. Martin's, 1977, pp. 107-135. Using a conversational style and layman's language and giving necessary lessons on astronomy along the way, Haldeman describes the planet Mercury in his chapter of a book that aims to bring up-to-date information on the solar system to general readers.

"This Space for Rent." *Analog*, November 1978, pp. 44-53. Haldeman writes about the space shuttle, "our first true spaceship:" the politics, business and science that have gone into its production, with some speculation on its possible effects. The article is adapted from *The Endless Horizon*, a non-fiction book of Haldeman's still in progress, which deals with space colonization.

X

ANNOTATED SECONDARY BIBLIOGRAPHY

Writings about Joe Haldeman are not yet available in great number. There have been several particularly thoughtful reviews of his fiction and a few published interviews with him. Often these articles appear in amateur science fiction magazines (fanzines), and the easiest method for finding them is to write directly to the fanzine. For that reason, addresses have been included where possible.

Budrys, Algis. "Books." Rev. of *Mindbridge* by Joe Haldeman. *The Magazine of Fantasy and Science Fiction*, April 1977, pp. 38-41. Budrys acknowledges Haldeman as one of the best of the new generation of science-fiction writers, finds his ideas (interstellar matter transmission, the mindbridge) full of dramatic potential that founders when he comes to discuss alien contact, and believes Haldeman's collage technique a skillful and witty way to make the story look better than it is.

Burk, James K. Rev. of *The Forever War* by Joe Haldeman. *Delap's F and SF Review* (P.O. Box 465721/W. Hollwood, CA 90046), June 1975, pp. 4-5. Burk sees the novel as the most realistic of the answers to Heinlein's *Starship Troopers*, written from the new perspective of the Vietnam war. He sees it as a well-written and promising first novel.

Isaacs, Leonard. "Books." Rev. of *The Forever War* by Joe Haldeman. *The Magazine of Fantasy and Science Fiction*, December 1975, pp. 38-40. For Isaacs, this novel, which treats war "as a personal and collective horror," is quite far from *Starship Troopers*. He is impressed by the "sharp-edged" writing, the gritty detail, the plausible science, and the social acumen of the book; he finds the battle and denouement at the end at variance with the tone of what went before.

McGuire, Patrick. "Variants: Joe Haldeman's SF Novels." *Algol* (P.O. Box 4175/New York, New York 10017), Summer-Fall 1977, pp. 19-20. McGuire establishes a structural and thematic pattern for Haldeman's novels and briefly examines the evolution of his works and his debt to Robert A. Heinlein.

McMurray, Clifford. "An Interview With Joe Haldeman." *Thrust: SF in Review* (P.O. Box 746/ Adelphi, MD 20783), Fall 1978, pp. 18-21. Haldeman discusses his attitudes to critical reception and awards, his writing routine, his use of Dos Passos' collage technique in *Mindbridge*, his plans for future writing projects.

March, Eric. "Joe Haldeman and the SF Alternative." *Starlog*, No. 17 (1978), pp. 45-47; Haldeman talks about writing, the message of science fiction, and alternate worlds.

Robinson, Spider. "Bookshelf." Rev. of *Mindbridge* by Joe Haldeman. *Galaxy*, December 1976, pp. 119-120. For Robinson, *Mindbridge* is a masterpiece: he finds it "the most mature study of telepathy since John Brunner's *The Whole Man*."

Samuelson, David. "*Locus* Looks at Books." Rev. of *Mindbridge* by Joe Haldeman. *Locus* (Box 3938/San Francisco, CA 94119), February 1977, p. 5. Samuelson sees *Mindbridge* as a sequel to *The Forever War*, padded with gimmickry from John Brunners's *Stand on Zanzibar* and too much symbolism. He finds *Mindbridge* annoyingly parodic of the military, of psychology, and of stock science-fiction motifs.

Sanders, Joe. Rev. of *Mindbridge* by Joe Haldeman. *Delap's F and SF Review* (P.O. Box 46572/ W. Hollywood, CA 90046) January 1977, pp. 24-25. Sanders also sees parallels to *The Forever War* but finds *Mindbridge* a strong hard science-fiction novel which shows people caught in social machinery and deals with how people cope with change.

Schweitzer, Darrell. "An Interview With Joe Haldeman." *Science Fiction Review* (P.O. Box 11408/ Portland, OR 97211), February 1977, pp. 26-30. Haldeman talks about his debt to Heinlein's *Starship Troopers*, his experience in and use of Vietnam, his attitude toward the art and craft of writing in and out of science fiction, and his writing methods.

Shippey, T.A. "Into Hell and Out Again." Rev. of *Mindbridge* by Joe Haldeman. *Times Literary Supplement*, 8 July 1977, p. 820. For Shippey, the great strength of *Mindbridge* is its use of multiple viewpoints, which he believes is a "good, hard-boiled way of telling a story about survival ethics."

Walker, Paul. "Bookshelf." Rev. of *All My Sins Remembered*. *Galaxy*, March 1978, pp. 138-140. Walker finds this novel typical of Haldeman's work insofar as it is too perfectly controlled. He admires the aliens of the first and third episodes but sees the second episode as inferior.

INDEX